DAYS OF CHAOS:
EMP Survival Series Book 2

JACK HUNT

DIRECT RESPONSE PUBLISHING

ISBN-13: 978-1985651319
ISBN-10: 1985651319

DAYS OF CHAOS

Also By Jack Hunt

The Renegades
The Renegades 2: Aftermath
The Renegades 3: Fortress
The Renegades 4: Colony
The Renegades 5: United
Mavericks: Hunters Moon
Killing Time
State of Panic
State of Shock
State of Decay
Defiant
Phobia
Anxiety
Strain
Blackout
Darkest Hour
Final Impact
And Many More…

Dedication

For my family.

Prologue

13 days after EMP

His leather jacket scrunched as he bent down over the gagged couple and lit a cigarette. In the darkness of the room, the small flame flickered, illuminating gasoline-drenched faces. Magnus Hobbs inhaled deeply and the end of the cigarette glowed a bright orange. The man and his wife whimpered watching the flame burn down the match until it went out.

"Look, I get it. I really do. You were just trying to protect your wife." He blew smoke into his face. "I can respect that, however, what I can't accept is rudeness. Now if you had just answered my question, you wouldn't be in this situation right now." He reached for a can of beer, taking another swig from it. "So if you want to blame anyone, blame yourself. You see, for every action we take in this life, there is a consequence. You made a call, and it backfired, didn't it?"

The man didn't answer. Not even a word.

Was it a final act of defiance or fear?

Magnus kept his eyes fixed on the man. Even in the dark he could register the familiar expression. They all had it. Of course they didn't start that way. Everyone was a hero until they were counting down the final minutes of their life.

He removed another match from the large box, struck it and waved it front of their faces, taunting them, and waiting for them to break — everyone did in the end.

The smell of gasoline lingered.

A muffled cry came from the woman.

He smiled, feeding off their terror.

"Magnus, we should get back," Sawyer said from behind him.

"Not until I get my answer."

"Cole's waiting for us."

"So? He can wait longer."

Sawyer leaned in and grabbed him by the jacket and he shrugged him off.

"Not until I get my answer," he repeated in a firm tone.

Sawyer shook his head and walked away.

Magnus looked back at the two and tilted his head and ran his hand over the wife's leg. Both of them were in their early twenties, and if the framed photos on the fireplace mantel were anything to go by, they were newlyweds. After not hearing back from Trent or Austin, and heading into Lake Placid to find out the state of things, they'd found their lifeless bodies, or what was left of them.

He'd grown up with both of them. They were his cousins, but felt more like brothers. When they entered Austin's home it stank to high heaven. They'd expected to find them riding out the EMP just like them. Instead he found both of them lying in the middle of their living room sporting gunshot wounds. Whoever killed them didn't even have the courtesy to bury them. It was almost like they were sending a warning to anyone who knew them. There was no note, no sign on the wall, no details, just the smell of death.

After they'd explored the house and taken in the sight of what remained of Lake Placid, he'd decided to drop by one of the neighbors to see what they could tell them. Magnus had no intention of it going this far. Contrary to what Cole and the others thought, he didn't get off on the suffering of others but after seeing how his kin had been treated, he sure as hell was ready to dish out punishment.

"Now I'm only going to ask you one more time. Who killed them?"

He leaned forward and pulled the gag down from the man.

"I told you, we don't know. There were a couple of break-ins along our street two weeks ago, and we heard someone was killed. My guess is your cousins murdered the man and someone retaliated. That's all I know. Now please, let us go."

"Let me guess, you won't say anything?"

He nodded.

Magnus's lips wormed into a smile before covering his mouth again with the gag.

"And what about you, darling?" He reached over and pulled her gag down. "You got anything else to add to that?"

She spit in his face. "Let us go, you pig."

He reached up and wiped her spit from his lower jaw and tasted it. "I have a good mind to drag you into the back and—"

"Magnus!" Sawyer hollered. "We need to go, there are people on the road with flashlights."

He eyed the woman and then covered her mouth with the gag. He rose to his feet and looked at them, shaking his head. "Utterly useless."

He crossed the living room heading toward the window so he could see. Sure enough outside there was a group of four armed men. In the two days they'd been in Lake Placid, they'd noticed that the town had some kind of neighborhood watch in place. They weren't cops as they were dressed like ordinary folk.

"We've been here long enough. It's time we head back and speak with him. Maybe he'll know what to do," Sawyer said.

Magnus eyed him. "Are you serious? The only thing he's going to do is a line of coke and lie around like he has for the past two weeks."

"They're gone, Magnus, and if we don't go soon, we might end up like them."

He glanced outside and observed the men going house to house. It wouldn't take them long and they'd be on the doorstep. He turned back toward the couple and Sawyer pulled at his arm. "Come on, leave them."

He headed toward the back door and Magnus followed.

After Sawyer exited, Magnus stood there for a second, then without any hesitation, he took out a match, lit it and dropped it. A blue flame crept across the floor, slithering its way toward the couple. Their muffled cries were the last thing he heard as he closed the door behind him.

Chapter 1

Lake Placid

They knew he was dead from the moment they walked in. Elliot Wilson stepped over the broken glass as he entered the home of Lake Placid Police Chief Derek Wayland. He hadn't been seen in several days and with a town of over two thousand people, and a limited number of vehicles old enough to operate, it had become tough checking on everyone's welfare. That's why Mayor Hammond had appointed neighborhood watch groups who were meant to do the rounds. Problem was, in light of dwindling resources, fewer people felt obliged to do anything.

Patrol Sergeant Gary Westin put a hand up to his nose. "That is rancid."

"Oh, you should smell the toilets in Rikers, now that's bad," Damon said.

It had been over two weeks since the EMP and the death toll was still climbing.

FEMA had been broadcasting updates on the situation, and Elliot's worst fear had come to fruition. The attack had come from North Korea. There were no details on how they'd managed to pull it off as FEMA's only concern was for the safety of Americans. Media reports leading up to the event had already stated how experts believed it could happen but people had underestimated the threat. FEMA had relayed that three high-altitude detonations had occurred in the upper atmosphere over California, Kansas and West Virginia and discussed how the weather would affect the power grid, crops, livestock and the water system. The problem was none of this was known until seventy-two hours after the event, leaving little time to alert the townsfolk. Under the circumstances they did the best they could by gathering together groups of ten or more people from different zones in the city and having them post flyers directing people to find the nearest concrete building, stay inside and get as far below ground as possible. Residents were instructed to stay inside for at least five days, fourteen was advisable but how long depended on multiple factors like the distance from the initial blast, wind direction, strength of the explosion and whether it hit the ground or detonated in the air. All they knew was West Virginia was over seven hundred miles away. What Elliot was able to make clear to the others was that up to 80 percent of the radiation reduced rapidly within the first twenty-four hours. Elliot had to assume that the winds must have worked in their favor because they were five hundred miles away in New York when the attack occurred, and none of them had experienced symptoms of radiation poisoning, something that he had feared from the moment the power grid went down. After making it back to Lake Placid, Elliot and the others had destroyed their clothes, bathed with shampoo and retreated to the safety of the bunker. Even though the two men who attempted to kill Rayna had destroyed the hinges on the shelter and lock, it didn't take long to patch it up and ensure the seal was airtight.

After twelve days of being inside and using a Geiger counter to assess radiation levels they felt it was safe to venture out. Outside it was far worse than they could imagine. Chaos was now in full swing. While some had heeded the advice and barricaded themselves inside their homes, others had chosen to take advantage of the opportunity and loot the pharmacies and grocery stores. Some had even broken into homes and killed others to take what they wanted. One of the first to die was Chief Derek Wayland.

They stood back observing his body. They'd gutted him like a fish. He was sprawled over the kitchen table with his entrails hanging out.

"You know what this means," Damon said slapping Gary on the back. "You're in charge now."

"Dear God, man, do you not have respect for the dead?" he shot back.

Damon raised an eyebrow. "Oh I'm sorry, was I meant to care?"

Through gritted teeth he spoke, "That's my friend."

"And?"

Gary shoved him up against the wall and before Elliot could intervene, Damon lashed out knocking him to the ground. "You touch me again, and it'll be the last time."

"Damon," Elliot said.

He threw a hand in the air. "Ah screw this." He trudged off out of the house, his boots crunching glass. The echo of a bucket being kicked across the lawn was the last they heard before it went quiet.

Elliot extended his hand and pulled Gary up.

"Seriously, Elliot, I don't know why you let him stay."

"Because of the fallout and…"

"And what? The guy is a known criminal."

"Yeah, well that criminal helped us get home."

Gary brushed himself off. It wasn't like the animosity between the two of them was strange. They'd been stuck inside that bunker for the past twelve days, and the tension between Gary and Damon wasn't the only thing he'd noticed. As they went about checking Wayland's home for anything that might be of use, Elliot thought back to the grueling days underground.

"I've been meaning to ask you. Did you notice the tension between Rayna and Jill?"

"No. Why?"

Elliot shrugged. "I dunno, I just noticed they kept their distance from each other and the few times they chatted it seemed cold like they were only doing it out of necessity."

"No idea," Gary said. "Maybe it was just stress. All of us have been a little stressed out."

He nodded. "Yeah, I guess."

They continued rooting through Wayland's home, thinking that perhaps Derek's death had been a retaliation of some form and not just an attempt to steal what he had. But it seemed by the looks of how bare his cupboards were, it was both. "You know we need to start thinking about water."

"There are enough streams around here, we should be fine."

"Yeah if you want to get waterborne diseases."

"The flyer we handed out already told people about disinfecting the water with purification tablets or adding 1 teaspoon of bleach to every 10 gallons of water."

"I'm not on about that, Gary, heck, fallout particles can't be removed from the water through just boiling or chemical disinfection, we need to look at the least radioactive sources such as wells, water tanks, covered reservoirs, seepage pits and deep lakes before we move on to ponds and streams. Most of the fallout particles settle at the bottom so the deeper the body of water, the safer it will be. Also bear in mind that we can use roof gutters because most of the particles would have run off with that downpour we had a few days back."

"If this stuff settled, we can't go drinking that," Gary said.

"I just told you, we've had showers since. Any fallout particles will have run off. What I'm saying is that we should at least give people the heads-up on how to remove fallout particles or dissolved radioactive material from water by using filtration through the earth's soil."

Gary turned and chuckled. "You always did pay better attention to this stuff than me."

They made their way out and took in the bright morning sun. After being stuck inside the bunker it had been a relief to step outside. It was January, still freezing cold. Much of the snow seemed to have melted, but that didn't mean there wouldn't be another drop in temperature. The east coast was notorious for changes in the weather, and they could go several days, even a week without snow, and then get hit again and find themselves digging themselves out of a hole. And rain? That just meant the sidewalks and roads would be hard to walk on.

"You know Damon was right. With Wayland gone this whole thing might fall on your shoulders."

"I think we are beyond who's in charge," Gary said. "But, no, Ted Murphy is the assistant chief. He'd be calling the shots."

Elliot snorted. "Well let's hope for your sake that's not the case."

Ted Murphy had been a pain in the ass for Gary for as long as they'd worked together. Before Elliot left for New York, Gary was always saying how Ted liked to exert his power over him. It probably didn't help that Gary had been in line for the assistant chief position and Ted had scooped it out from underneath him by making up some bull crap story that had made Gary look incompetent.

The radio on Gary's chest crackled.

"Come in, Gary, this is Foster. You might want to see this."

Gary pushed the button on his radio and brought it to his lips. "Go ahead, over."

Static came over the line and then Foster Goodman responded. "We headed over to that house that was on fire yesterday, looks like I've found the cause."

Foster Goodman worked with the local fire department as the fire marshal and though they were limited by what they could do (and right now that meant letting fires burn out), Gary wanted to at least know what the cause was. There had been a surge of fires prior to going underground and even more since coming up topside — it made them believe that it was being used as a distraction while other homes were being raided. The department didn't want to waste their time attending every blaze especially when their resources were already spread so thin, so Foster and a few of the guys were tackling it as best as they could.

Foster continued. "We got two dead bodies. Whoever did this must have soaked them in an accelerant. That's just my determination based on the pattern of the fire."

Gary went quiet. Elliot could see him wrestling with the new burden. Towns and cities all over the country had to have been in the same position.

"What do you want us to do?" Foster asked.

Gary shifted one foot to the next casting a glance across the yard to Damon who was sitting on a swing. Chief Wayland had been divorced for some time. All that remained of his family life was a rusted swing set and a few photos. According to Gary, his ex had taken his daughter to live in Saranac Lake. His son had already passed away in a car crash. Elliot shook his head as he looked at a photo of the family. Death was the new reality.

"Just continue your rounds and report back on those additional fires."

"Sergeant, my guys are tired and we are down to only two right now. The rest have gone home. They're concerned about finding food, and water, and they're not alone."

"Alright, just do what you can," Gary replied. He released the button on his radio and walked over to where Elliot and Damon were waiting. In the first twenty-four hours after emerging from the bunker Gary and Elliot had gone around to the homes of officers, volunteers, and including the mayor, and set about visiting the grocery stores and pharmacies to see if there was anything left to salvage.

Fortunately, most of the nonperishable food had already been taken and stored inside the Olympic Center which was being used as a shelter and guarded by two armed officers who opted to sleep there. Unfortunately, when they emerged from the bunker the found the desperate had broken off the locks, lifted shutters and broken windows to steal the rest. With no power, there were no alarms and with almost everyone inside their homes it wasn't a surprise to find most of the food gone from the grocery stores.

The next order of business was to protect what they had by setting up roadblocks to the north, south, east and west. So far, there didn't appear to be many folks town-hopping but Elliot knew eventually that it would happen as supplies dwindled in surrounding towns. Hell, they'd even thought about taking a trip into Keene or Saranac Lake and seeing what the situation was like there.

The barricades would be manned by volunteers to prevent outsiders from entering and to ensure the protection of the town as there was no telling who was starting these fires or who had raided the grocery stores and two pharmacies. It was an overwhelming task due to a lack of manpower and not everyone wanted to help.

And the situation would only get worse as people began to gossip among themselves about what was being done. Once they realized they were shit out of luck, people would take matters into their own hands.

"You want to head over to see Foster?" Elliot asked.

"No, I need to go speak with Ted. Find out how he wants to handle things."

Elliot rested a hand against the doorframe. "You know you don't need his permission, Gary."

"Until we see a complete breakdown of order in this town, we will continue to operate and abide by the laws that governed us before the EMP."

Elliot chuckled. "Listen to yourself. You've really bought into this shit, haven't you? Did Hammond say that? Look around you, Gary. You know as well as I do that we are beyond the point of maintaining order. It's every man for himself now," he said hopping into the 1970s green Jeep. It roared to life and Gary rode shotgun while Damon got in the back.

"Just drop me off at the department. Others might

27

have quit but I'm not. Not yet."

Elliot held his tongue. Gary was a true patriot, the kind of man that would have gone down with a sinking ship rather than abandon it. He admired that but at the same time he thought it was naïve. Clearly in the past few days, certain residents, thugs or gangs had made it painfully obvious that they no longer would abide by the rules. And anyway, who was going to enforce them? There was already a lack of manpower and some of the people who had originally helped before, were now gone. They'd abandoned the town, probably wised up to the fact that if they stayed they would have felt under obligation to help.

For some the challenges facing the town were too great to handle. The only reason Elliot had agreed to go along with him that morning was because he was hoping to sway Gary's mindset and get him on board with ideas he had about their own survival; some of which would involve stepping over the line between that which was right and wrong.

After dropping Gary off, Elliot headed back up Mirror Lake Drive to check in with Rayna. Before that he planned to stop by the home of Michael and Stephanie.

Once Gary was gone Damon climbed from the back to the front.

"You know your buddy's a real dick."

"And you're not?" Elliot asked.

"What?"

"If I have to answer that, there's no point in talking."

Damon nodded. "Alright. I get it. I was a little insensitive back there, but he's living in a fantasy if he thinks that this town or country is going to bounce back from this. And yet he's rallying up the troops as though this is nothing more than a downed line. It's bullshit."

Elliot glanced at several neighbors and made a passing gesture to them.

"He'll come around."

"You sure about that?" Damon replied.

Elliot shook his head and veered into the driveway that led up to the smoldering mess. To his surprise, Foster

Goodman was still outside along with two guys from the fire department. One guy was leaning up against a vehicle, smoking a cigarette, and the other was sitting on the back drinking a beer.

"See, I told you," Damon said, pointing out the obvious. Elliot swerved in and killed the engine. He hopped out and went over to Foster.

"You want to show me the bodies."

He looked Elliot up and down and then nodded before tossing him a mask for the fumes. On the way in, Foster told him to mind his step. "Been a while since I've seen you in town. Where were you?"

Elliot ignored him as he guided him through the charred remains. The fire was still going in some areas while the rest smoldered away. As they made their way to the back of the house, he caught sight of the young couple. They were gripping each other tight and their bodies were burned beyond comprehension.

Foster lifted his mask for a second and spat a thick wad of phlegm nearby. "Poor bastards. Terrible way to go."

Elliot closed his eyes and had a flashback of his friend inside the armored personnel carrier. The flames flickering, his skin melting, the screams and the final moments of his life.

"Elliot. Elliot!" Foster shook him by the arm and he snapped out of it. "You okay?"

He nodded and turned, making his way back to the Jeep. He tossed the mask back to Foster and hopped inside without saying another word. But that didn't stop Damon from opening his trap.

"You guys should get back to work, my taxes aren't paying you to sit around. Don't you have fires to put out?" He smirked and one of the guys flipped him the bird.

Before Elliot could pull away, Foster ambled over to them. He spat another wad of phlegm and wiped his lips with the back of his hand.

"Oh, I forgot to tell Gary. We spoke with some of your neighbors across the way that were out that night doing rounds," he said. "Seems they saw two men running through the woods not long after the flames appeared. One of the guys took off after them but couldn't catch a license plate. So it's hard to know if it was locals but he saw them drive off in what he believes was a sky blue 1979 Scout with a white stripe down the side." He tossed up a hand. "Maybe that will help."

Elliot gave a nod. "I'll be sure to pass that along."

Chapter 2

Jesse looked over the shopping list Elliot had given him before leaving. Had he remained in New York he wouldn't have thought about taking any precautionary measures. That morning he and Maggie had been out gathering what they could from local hardware stores. Jesse had no idea what the town looked like before they crawled into the shelter but after driving up Saranac Avenue heading for Aubuchon Hardware they could tell that the world they'd left behind had changed drastically and not for the better. He'd borrowed a 1983 Ford Bronco from Mr. Thompson. Apparently he hadn't taken it out of his garage in over a year. The thing was his pride and joy and he was a little apprehensive about letting them use it but Rayna had sweet-talked him into it because the goods they were bringing back were going to benefit him as well. It would require a few trips back and forth so they needed the space.

"Alright, shout it out," Maggie said shuffling down an aisle with a shopping cart. Someone had already been inside the store to gather a few items, but it wasn't in as bad a state as the grocery store they'd passed on the way up. Now that place was a wreck. Shelves had been cleared out, windows were smashed and someone had set the back half of the store on fire.

"Poly sandbags, barbed wire, black plastic bags, driveway spikes…"

"Whoa, slow down," she said, pushing the cart then hopping on the back and coasting down the aisle toward him. "How about your give me half of that sheet and you get the rest?"

He shrugged. "Suits me fine."

Jesse tore the paper in half and set off to find another cart. He continued talking. "You know why he wants all this stuff?"

"To fortify the property."

"Why? If people want in they're getting in."

"Yeah but you don't want to make it easy for them."

Jesse eyed the shelf and grabbed up six rolls of barbed wire and threw them in the cart, then scooted over to the other side and grabbed up some plastic bags.

"You think he's a little paranoid?"

"You heard what Rayna said about those two men. I think he just wants to look out for them."

"That's what worries me," Jesse replied. "Makes me think his hospitality will soon run out."

He continued on down to another aisle collecting what was on the list and talking to her as they went. She was three aisles over. Occasionally they would spot each other through the shelves. Leaving New York hadn't been easy and some might have said that he was crazy to have left with strangers but in the short time he'd got to know them they felt more like family than anything else. The problem wasn't that he didn't know them; instead it was the fact that society created an environment that kept everyone at arm's length. Some days in New York he could have gone a whole day without talking to someone, or even making eye contact.

"Oh this is perfect," Jesse said stepping back from thin wooden boards that were going to be used as warning signs throughout the neighborhood. Elliot wanted to erect signs that said: NOTHING INSIDE IS WORTH DYING FOR. "Maggie, tell me something. You believe in fate?"

"Like events unfolding that are beyond our control?" she hollered back.

"Yeah. This whole event has got me thinking. I mean, what are the chances that we would meet each other? I mean, all four of us." He was mostly referring to her but he wasn't planning on saying it out loud. It hadn't taken long, two weeks to be exact, to be drawn to her. And if he was honest she been part of the reason why he left New York. Of course he wasn't going to tell her that, not yet. Not while tensions were riding high and everyone's minds were occupied with survival.

She never responded and so he continued loading up his cart with one item after the other: stainless steel bird spikes, safety window film, dummy dome cameras, door security guards, striker plates, door jammers, nails and... He stopped the cart realizing he hadn't heard her move in several minutes.

"Maggie!"

There was no response. He reached for a hammer off the shelf and shoved it into his waistband and covered it with his top. He then swung around the Winchester lever rifle and made his way around the corner. Jesse stopped every couple of feet to listen for footsteps but he couldn't hear anything. No talking. No movement. He wanted to call out to her but that would have given away his location and right now that was all he had going for him. His eyes darted around walls looking for the dome mirrors that security and staff used to keep an eye on customers as they browsed products. His heart started beating faster as he came around the next aisle, to find it empty barring her cart. "Maggie!" He couldn't take it anymore. He yelled out her name moving fast down the aisles. Just as he was getting closer to the last two aisles he spotted movement in the mirrored dome. Jesse ducked.

There were two men, and one of them had a hold of her. He could just make him out, a grizzled-looking guy, mid-forties, wearing a thick winter jacket and gloves. He had a hand over Maggie's mouth while the other guy was making his way down the aisle heading in his direction. He exhaled trying to stay calm. He knew what he had to do. Elliot had already gone over it with them while they were in the shelter. His mind flashed back to his frequent talks about being ready to kill if it came down to it. *I don't care how good you think your aim is. Don't get cocky. No headshots. Aim for the chest or stomach. It's the largest area of the body and chances are you are going to hit that before you nail a headshot.*

It wasn't like this kill would be his first. He thought for a second or two about the man he'd killed on the way into Essex County. That night had changed everything for him. He'd stepped over the line and there was no coming back from that. His eyes flitted to the mirror as he darted out and skirted around into aisle three. If he killed the one, but didn't manage to get the other, there was a good chance Maggie would die. He moved quickly from one end of the aisle down to the other preparing for the man to swing around the end into his field of vision. There was a fifty-fifty chance of being killed. He knew that, and that was why he took a small can of paint off the shelf and rolled it across the ground into another aisle, then waited for the man to turn. One second, that was all he needed, just a momentary distraction.

Jesse focused on the dome mirror, pressing his back into the shelf. As the tin can hit the shelving unit, it clattered. The man twisted around, and Jesse swung the rifle out and squeezed off a round.

The echo was deafening. The round struck him in the gut sending him down. Jesse hurried forward and finished him off with another to the heart before ducking back into the aisle. He heard a voice call out.

"Doug!"

He knew he had seconds.

Jesse hurried down the aisle staying low until he could see the lower half of the man's body. He rested the rifle on the shelf and was in the process of placing his finger on the trigger when the guy moved. *No!*

He shifted position and tried to spot him but he was out of sight.

A round went off and he thought the guy had shot Maggie but when he glanced at the mirror, he realized what he'd done. He'd shattered the mirror so Jesse couldn't see him.

"Boy! If you want to walk out of this store alive you will listen to me very carefully. Put the rifle down, and the keys to the truck and walk away."

"Let her go," Jesse yelled back. "And you can have whatever you want."

"No, she's staying right here."

"C'mon man, you don't need to do this," Jesse replied.

"You're not listening, are you? Now put the gun and keys down and walk out."

"Look, if it's supplies you want. You can take ours. But let her go."

He heard him snort. "Doug! Doug, you there?"

The man wasn't going to get any response from his friend. He was bleeding out three aisles down. What he thought was a gun in his hand had actually been a machete. Jesse figured they wanted their rifles. Guns and ammo were now the new currency. Forget trading. It all came down to what they were slinging. Trading had no place when a person was looking down the barrel of a gun.

* * *

Maggie didn't stand a chance. Moments earlier she'd walked right into him when she came around the end of the aisle. Before she could pull the rifle off her back the brawny guy had clamped his hand over her mouth and yanked her head back causing agony in her throat.

It happened so fast.

Now she stood close to him with a blade pressed against her jugular, and a hand gripping her hair. She'd reeled through some of the basic self-defense moves Rayna had taught her but in that moment she couldn't think clear enough to remember. However, she knew that if she didn't do something fast there was a chance both of them would die.

"Doug!"

She swallowed hard feeling the steely blade press hard into her larynx.

Her mind went back to what Rayna had said as she stood behind Maggie with a blade to her throat and showing her how to get out from it.

If someone holds a knife to your throat from behind, you don't have many options. The biggest mistake people make is to try and pull the knife away but that can actually help your attacker. If opportunity is there, you want to bring up your arms slowly, then latch on to that knife hand, pull it down from your body and duck your left shoulder and draw yourself out. But remember, if you don't do it right, you will die.

Rayna had made it sound so easy and back when she was showing her it was. They'd practiced several times a day because there was very little to do in the shelter except read, play board games and listen to the radio. Perhaps that's why she'd started to bond with Jesse. She got a sense that he liked her by the way she'd catch him looking at her from time to time. While relationships weren't her strong point, knowing when a guy was interested was.

"I'm going to count to ten, if you don't put your rifle down and come around now, your girlfriend will taste blood," her attacker said.

Jesse was trying to reason with him, give him any other option but this guy wasn't listening. He knew what he wanted and he wasn't ready to walk away until he got it. In her head Maggie started counting along with the man. When he reached five she would attempt to do what Rayna had taught her. There was no other choice.

"2... 3... 4..."

She was about to react when the crack of a gun went off near her ear. It sounded so loud she didn't even register the man dropping to the ground. One second he was holding her tight, the next he slumped to the floor with blood seeping out of his skull. There was ringing in her ears. She stumbled forward, then reached for the gun immediately just in case he wasn't dead. Maggie backed up and looked at the blood forming a puddle around his head. Right then Jesse came around the corner, slinging his rifle over his shoulder and hurrying toward her. He gripped her with both hands.

"You okay?"

It took her a few seconds to respond because the noise had rattled her.

He shook her. "Maggie."

"Besides the ringing in my ears? I think so." She crouched down and took a moment to gather her thoughts. "How did you know where he was?"

"I didn't initially until I heard him shift."

"So you just took the shot?"

"Pretty much."

She turned and batted him a few times around the head.

"You could have killed me, you fool!"

"Whoa, hold up, princess. I just saved your damn life."

"Yeah because you were lucky."

He chuckled but she wasn't laughing. She didn't look at him.

"Look, Maggie. I could see his feet. I had a rough idea of where he was. It was enough to take the shot. From the last view I got of him he was head and shoulders above you. I aimed high."

"Oh, well now you put it that way." She shook her head in disbelief. "Is the other one dead?"

"Yeah." He frowned. "Are you sure you're okay?"

She swallowed hard then pointed the gun at the man.

Jesse pressed down on the barrel. "It's over, he's dead."

"I know but..." she trailed off still in shock. "I just want to know what it feels like to squeeze the trigger on someone."

He scoffed. "Your time will come, Maggie, but believe me, it doesn't get any easier and until it happens you don't want to deal with the crap that comes with it. Come on, let's get what we came for and get the hell out of here."

Jesse gathered up the men's two steel machetes and

one pack of smokes before carting out what they had to the truck. Jesse opened the steel enclosure and filled it with as much as they could, then closed it up and piled the rest on top, tying it all together with elastic bungee cord hooks.

The Bronco rumbled as they made their way back home and Maggie replayed the final moment of the man's life. She'd never been that close to someone when they'd died. She gazed down at her hands and noticed she had blood on them. Ever since the event had started she'd been thinking about what she was going to do when it came down to pulling the trigger on someone. Could she do it? She hoped so.

Chapter 3

Cole Tucker sat alone at a glass table inside Baxter Mountain Tavern. In front of him were eight plates of the finest food off the menu. Most of it had been consumed; some portions had been picked at. At that exact moment, Cole was tucking into a nice juicy Black Angus New York strip steak. He closed his eyes and savored every bite. Lying a few feet away on the ground were two dead state troopers. It didn't faze him one bit. He stopped chewing to wipe his lips with a napkin and take a sip of red wine. He looked at the bottle and tossed it around in his hands. It was valued at over eighty dollars. Certainly not the kind of liquor he was used to consuming before the shit hit the fan.

Devin and Tyron sat at the bar knocking back beers and shooting the breeze while a nervous chef sat in a chair a few tables down waiting for his marching orders. They'd dragged him out of his house and brought him down to the tavern located not far from the main stretch.

"I've got to say, Pete, you outdid yourself this time. My preference is the steak but those pork chops — wow! What did you put on those?"

His lip quivered with fear. "Rosemary and garlic."

"And what about the Sausage Trio?"

"Pheasant Cognac."

He squinted at him and shook his knife. "Come on now, Pete, I got a hint of onion in there."

"There were caramelized onions."

He snorted. "I knew it."

Tyron hopped over the bar and took several glasses and lined them up then opened a bottle of whiskey and began pouring it from high above letting it splash between the glasses as he filled them.

Devin turned on his stool eyeing Pete. "Where are the owners?"

Pete shrugged.

When they'd arrived three hours ago the place was locked and empty. In fact most of the stores in Keene were like that in the days after the power went out. At first Cole had been cautious; they'd seen power outages before with the longest lasting nine hours but nothing compared to this. Whatever had caused this had sent society into panic mode. They initially tried to get answers from neighbors and those still in town but everyone was in the same boat. They had no clue. And being as the town had less than a thousand people, options were limited on where they could go to find out information. When it came to public services, there was the town hall which dealt with tickets and small claims but that was the extent of it. Then there was the health center, a church, two banks, a post office, one school and a library. Beyond that were a couple of supermarkets but that was it. It was a shithole in the middle of nowhere and didn't offer much in the way of resources. Most folks headed to Lake Placid or Saranac Lake if they needed anything.

It didn't take long in those first five days for lawlessness to run rampant. Eventually when police didn't show up, he figured they had their hands full, so he joined those who were looting. Of course they took things to the next level and executed a few who were making off with some good shit but in his book that was par for the course. This was all about survival of the fittest and if anyone was going to remain standing, it was him.

After breaking into the tavern that morning he didn't want to go through all the hassle of whipping up food when he knew exactly where the chef lived. Dragging his ass out of bed had scared his wife and kids shitless but he promised no harm would come to him and he would have him back in one piece before the clock struck twelve.

And he meant it.

He'd known Pete for over twenty years. Like many living in Keene, Pete was born and raised there and had operated like any other law-abiding citizen until all hell broke loose.

"You worried about your family?" Cole asked.

Pete nodded.

"Well don't — we're gonna take good care of you Pete

and make sure your family survive. Are you running low on supplies?"

He frowned, opened his mouth and then closed it.

"It's okay, speak up. I'm not going to bite." Cole pointed to the two dead officers on the ground. "I know that's a little disconcerting but I did you and me a favor."

Pete looked confused. Cole enjoyed educating people, it gave him a sense that he was doing his part, giving back and well, ensuring that he didn't have to deal with dumb questions later.

"You see now, if I'd allowed them to take me in, you wouldn't go home this evening with a whole stack of food, now would you?"

He shrugged slightly but looked as if Cole was asking a trick question.

Cole gestured to Devin. "Go gather a box of peaches, rice, potatoes and throw in a few bottles of wine and give it to our man here. He deserves it."

Cole observed his reaction. There was a lot that he could gauge by a man's reaction to kindness. He could tell if they were going to be a problem later or someone he could rely on. And right now for them to build what he had in mind he needed more people capable of seeing the bigger picture. His mind had already begun to think of the numerous ways they could benefit. Charging a toll on the roads, turning the town into a camp where they could bring in those of value like Pete and use them. It was all about careful manipulation. Give a little, take a lot. He's used the same principle when drug dealing. He bought coke at rock-bottom pricing and turned around and charged a fortune, except before he did that he would hand out small baggies to get people hooked on it. They would appreciate his generosity and on occasion he would do it again.

As he returned to eating, a truck came barreling toward the tavern and stopped several yards from the wall. Sawyer hopped out the drivers side wearing a big grin. He made his way inside.

"Guys!" Sawyer said.

Devin turned on his stool. "What did you bring back?"

"Nothing for you," Sawyer replied. "But we do have a truck full of goods."

Cole noticed when Magnus got out he didn't have the same expression on his face. Cole continued chewing and leaned back in his seat feeling overly full. Who said people needed to starve when government screwed up? He had no intentions of going hungry. In his eyes the future looked bright with no one governing his actions and no one setting the standard for how he should live. Magnus ambled in and eyed Cole. It was like someone had sucked out whatever energy was in him. He wasn't like that when he left.

"Tyron, Devin, take Pete home."

"But we haven't eaten yet," Tyron complained.

"Take a plate with you and do as you're told."

Tyron came around the bar and scooped up a couple of plates and gestured for Pete to follow them out.

"And remember, Pete. There is more where that came from. All I ask in return is you cook a meal or two every now and again. Sound good?"

He nodded and headed out.

Sawyer leaned across the bar and scooped up one of the glasses Tyron had poured and downed it. He hopped onto a stool and lit a cigarette, then blew out smoke. His eyes darted between Magnus and Cole.

"Magnus. Come take a seat," Cole said, gesturing to a chair.

He strolled over and slipped in across from him.

"So? Did you find him?" he continued.

"I saw Damon, yeah. But Trent and Austin." He dipped his head.

Cole leaned forward and grabbed a hand around the back of his head. "You can tell me."

"They're dead. Both of them were shot."

"Suicide?"

He bristled. "No. Why would you think that?"

"Well Trent wasn't that bright. Now was he?"

That set him off. "He was a good man."

"Magnus, he fucked up numerous times. And now you find him dead and you're surprised?"

He sat back in his seat and looked at Sawyer. "Throw us a glass."

Sawyer jumped over the bar and grabbed up an empty glass and tossed it. Cole caught it and placed it in front of Magnus. He began filling. When he reached the top he continued to pour. The exquisite red wine spilled over and created a puddle.

"What are you doing?" Magnus asked.

Cole leaned back and filled his own glass. The alcohol was kicking in and making him feel relaxed and at ease.

"You see that," he said pointing to the overfilled glass. "That's now." He then pointed to his own glass that was only half full. "That's before all of this happened."

Magnus shook his head while Cole lit a cigarette. "What the hell are you on about?"

"You don't see it, do you, Magnus?" Cole asked.

"See what?"

"When you were in Lake Placid, what did you see?"

"People dead on the streets, neighbors patrolling, a lack of police and… fear," he trailed off looking forlorn.

"That's not what you saw."

"I know what I fucking saw." He leaned forward and scooped up the glass, wine spilling over, and chugged it down.

"It wasn't fear. Its opportunity," Cole said.

He could tell Magnus didn't understand. He looked over at Sawyer who was smiling. He'd always been the quickest to catch on to what Cole meant. Cole leaned back and put his feet up and inhaled deeply the nicotine as he gazed out the large window at the road.

"Right now everyone is scared. Emergency services are barely hanging on by a thread. Some towns don't even have any. People are lost. Desperate. And you know what that means?"

"We're gonna die?" Magnus said, taking another swig of his wine.

"No. We're gonna thrive, Magnus. It means they are in need of a shepherd. Someone to lead them, feed them and give them the false security blanket that the government once gave." He breathed in deeply. "And we're the ones that are going to do it."

He scoffed. "Oh like we were going to take over the drug game and yet we only dealt in Keene because you were too damn chicken shit to branch out into Lake Placid?"

As Magnus turned to eye Sawyer and smirk, Cole lunged forward and grabbed him by the head and slammed his face into a plate of sesame encrusted tuna. Then with the other hand he pressed his Glock into the side of his temple.

"You listen to me. The reason we are still alive is because of me. The reason you aren't rotting inside some hellhole is because of me. Show some damn respect. Don't ever mistake patience for a lack of courage. Do you hear me?"

"Yeah, I got it," he said spitting tuna.

"What's that?"

"I got it!" he yelled.

"Good."

Cole released him and sat back eyeing him just in case

he decided to lay down a few haymakers. It wouldn't have been the first time he'd ended up in a brawl with him. Their work prior to the lights going out had placed them in stressful situations and it had a way of bringing out the worst in them. He just wanted to make sure he knew his place. He tossed a napkin at him. "Now wipe that shit off your face."

He downed what was left in his glass. "As I was saying before you rudely interrupted. The opportunity before us presents some challenges but as you can tell," he cast his gaze at the two state troopers, "we are more than ready for what it brings. Now we start small with this town. We get twenty, thirty, fifty people onboard and it won't be long before we're running Essex County."

"And the cops?" Sawyer said.

He closed his eyes. "Did I not just explain that?"

"Yeah but that's here. State Police have a larger ground to cover but Lake Placid has local officers."

"Sure. But so does Saranac Lake. We begin here, Sawyer, and once we have enough people on our side, it doesn't matter how many there are."

Sawyer nodded.

"And what about my cousins?" Magnus said still wiping his face.

"We'll deal with it. You have my word."

"When?"

He flashed him another look of death. Magnus raised his hands. "I'm just asking, man."

"Soon. In the meantime we have work to do here."

"People are on edge, Cole," Sawyer said.

"So we give them a reason to relax."

"They're scared and — " Magnus began to add.

"So we give them a reason to not be," Cole cut him off.

"They're hungry."

He studied his face. "So we feed them."

Their brows knit together. Uncertain. Doubtful even. It was to be expected, they were in new territory, but the way Cole saw it this was no different from dealing, except the drugs had changed. Now the drugs were safety, food, water, sleep, shelter and a few others.

"Where do we begin?"

"By giving them a taste. Small steps. We'll start with a handful of people and each day increase it. Give it a few weeks, a month or two and we'll have enough people with us to not only protect what we have built here but enough to take what others have built elsewhere."

"I don't know about that," Magnus said, shaking his head. Cole narrowed his eyes. "I'm not disagreeing, I'm just saying it seems like a lot of work to earn people's trust when we can just take what we need."

"And what happens when others come? And they will. What then? There are five of us right now. It's enough to survive for the short term but we need to think about the long term. Those lights aren't coming back on. Those gas stations aren't going to be refueled. Those grocery shelves aren't going to be stocked. To take what we need, requires manpower. And nothing works better to hook people in than giving them a little something in return." He glanced at both of them. "We share now so we can control later. That's how society has always done it. Now it's our turn."

Magnus nodded. "And what about Damon?"

"You say you saw him?"

"With a group of people. He didn't look like he had plans on returning here."

Cole tapped the table with his fingers and rocked back in his seat. Why hadn't he shown up here? His girl was here. His family was here. They were here. "Well I guess it's time we had a little reunion."

Chapter 4

"You knew them?" Elliot bellowed pointing an accusing finger at Damon. They were standing outside his home in the driveway. Behind him a cold wind made the branches of an old oak sway under a gray sky. Damon was on one side of the Jeep while Elliot was on the other. He'd been unusually quiet on the journey back to the house. At first Elliot thought he was still pissed at Gary but then he'd blurted it out. Apparently, unbeknownst to them, Damon thought he knew who was behind the killing of his neighbors.

"Why didn't you tell us?" Elliot asked.

"I was going to but there never seemed to be a good time."

"Bullshit," Elliot shot back. "We were in that bunker for twelve days."

"And I was a guest," Damon said.

"Yeah, damn right you were." He tossed a hand up. "I

fed you and made sure you were protected."

"You didn't have to."

"No, I didn't." He scoffed. "You didn't say anything because you didn't want to get kicked out, did you?"

"Elliot, I only recognized one of them."

"Which one?"

"Trent — the one who attacked Rayna."

Elliot ran a hand over his face. He couldn't believe he was telling him this. Since entering the shelter he hadn't said a word. Would it have changed things? Maybe.

"Look, I don't know if they're behind the death of your neighbors but when Foster mentioned a sky blue 1979 Scout with a white stripe down the side. It got me thinking."

"It got you thinking, did it?"

Rayna must have noticed how long it was taking them to enter and stepped out to see if everything was okay. Her eyes bounced between them. "Everything okay, Elliot?"

"Yeah, just go inside, I'll only be a minute."

She was hesitant, then nodded and went back in. Elliot walked around to the rear of the Jeep to unload a few supplies he had collected from an abandoned home on the east side. It was mostly plywood, aluminum fencing and a steel box of tools. He figured it could come in handy for when they started securing the property. He took a seat on the back bumper and tapped out a cigarette. Damon glanced at him. Usually he would have offered him one but in the foul mood he was in, and after what he'd just told him, he didn't give him one.

"Well?" Elliot asked. "How do you know him?"

Damon leaned against the Jeep. "He's the cousin of a friend of mine back in Keene. I only saw him a few times when Magnus brought him out to chat to Cole." He breathed in deeply and looked off toward the mouth of the driveway. "He was a small-time dealer, operating here. Magnus was trying to persuade Cole to expand his operation to include Lake Placid."

"Selling drugs."

He nodded.

Elliot shook his head in disbelief at how he'd gone all this time without saying a word. "Well that explains how you wound up in Rikers." He ran a hand over his knee and took a hard drag on the cigarette. "Are you sure the vehicle belongs to this... Magnus guy?" Elliot asked.

"I'm not sure but Cole, the friend of mine, owned one. He runs a garage, and he'd purchased one about six years ago. It was sky blue with a white stripe down the side."

"You think they were responsible for Chief Wayland's death?"

Damon shrugged. "No idea. But if it is Magnus, he won't stop until he finds out who killed his cousin. Him and Trent were like brothers."

Elliot placed his hand on the grip of his holstered weapon and withdrew it. Damon took a cautionary step back.

"Settle down. I'm not gonna shoot you," Elliot said without looking at him. He pulled out the magazine and began adding a few more bullets to it. Earlier that morning they'd run into a bit of trouble on the east side.

Nothing they couldn't handle but he had to fire off a few warning shots in the air to ward off an antagonist group. They, along with others, had stopped them on their way over to Chief Wayland's home, presumably to lighten their load. Of course, he'd expected residents to be outside looking for food and taking matters into their own hands now they were two weeks in. It would only get worse from here on out.

"Yeah, that would be a bit extreme," Damon replied, his mouth curling into a smile. "Look, I need to head back to Keene. My girl is there."

"You never told me you had one."

"You never asked."

There was some truth in that. He hadn't really taken the time to get into deep discussions with Damon. Jesse, on the other hand had, but there was a reason for that. Elliot had spent a large majority of those twelve days talking with Rayna. She was more forgiving of him than he was of himself. Though he could tell the dynamics between the two of them had changed. She was cautious and had every right to be. After walking out on her and the children, he was surprised that she even let him back in. But that was Rayna. A woman with a heart of gold. She'd always been the one to see the glass half full. The kids, well they were kids, quick to forgive and just glad to have their dad back. He expected them to be clingy, but it was quite the opposite. In the year he'd been away, they had no other choice than to grow up fast.

"Besides, it's a bit of an off-and-on relationship. Hell, I'm not even sure if she'll be around."

Elliot nodded. "I understand."

Silence stretched between them.

"I'll find out what's going on and if they were responsible."

"So you're thinking of coming back?"

He looked at Elliot and frowned. "You know when I left New York, I had no intention of staying in Lake Placid but after everything, and the dangers of fallout, I just figured it would make sense to stay put until it was safe to come out. I don't know if I'll return, or if I'll stay in Keene. I just know I have to go and speak to Cole and see my girl. If I can find out what happened in the process, I owe you that."

"You don't owe me anything."

"Maybe you don't think I do but..."

As he was talking, tires squealed as the truck driven by Jesse pulled into the lot, a plume of white smoke swirled up behind it into the chilly air. It sounded like it was on its last legs. They were lucky to find another vehicle. Gary said they couldn't keep them because the department needed them. Elliot had mixed feelings about that. It wasn't that he didn't want the police to be able to do their job, but he felt they had bitten off more than they could chew. Jesse parked it at an angle behind the Jeep and hopped out. He slammed the door and gave it a kick.

"What a piece of shit!"

"Did the job though," Elliot said.

When Maggie got out she had this sheepish look on her face.

"What's up?" Damon asked.

"Besides the vehicle having a mind of its own?" Jesse said staring down at his blackened hands that were covered in grease. "Damn thing gave up the ghost ten minutes from Aubuchon Hardware." He slapped the top of the hood.

"We ran into a spot of trouble," Maggie replied walking to the back of the truck and beginning to haul out some items. Elliot went over to give them a hand.

"Two guys," Jesse said. "Wanted the truck and our rifles."

"And?" Elliot replied reaching into the back and pulling out an armful of barbed wire rolls. "You handled it?"

"I had no choice."

"We always have a choice," Elliot said casting a glance at Damon.

He then noticed blood on Maggie's face. "You hurt?"

She shook her head. "I'm fine. Just a little shaken up."

* * *

Damon could feel the tension building between them

as he assisted hauling in the goods. He didn't blame Elliot for his reaction. Had he been in the same position he would have probably said the same thing. He really was planning on telling them but with all the commotion, and Rayna's wounds being treated, he didn't think it was worth it. There was also the fact that he hadn't planned on staying so he assumed what they didn't know wouldn't hurt them. But after seeing the charred remains of Elliot's neighbors and hearing the description of the vehicle, he had to say something, if only to get it off his chest. There was no way of telling for sure if it was them but he knew Magnus and what he was capable of. He thought Cole had a short fuse but Magnus, well, he bordered on psychotic. His thoughts drifted back to one time in Keene when they'd been out drinking at a local bar. A random stranger had bumped into Magnus and spilled his beer. He apologized and even offered to buy him another, but he declined and over the course of the next hour sat there brooding, staring at the guy and his girlfriend until they left the bar. Seconds after, he said he had to make a phone call. When he returned he had blood all over his knuckles and a relieved look on his face as if he'd just exorcised his inner demons. And the insane part? Anyone else would have left the bar, not Magnus. Nope, he waited for the cops to show up and by then he was full of liquid courage and ready to rumble. It took three of them to drag his ass out of that bar. He was deranged that was for sure.

Once the final item was removed from the back of the truck, Damon approached Jesse and asked if he could get a ride.

"You leaving us?" Jesse asked.

Damon looked over to Elliot who was talking with Rayna. Maggie walked over, her face now clean.

"I think I've stayed long enough. I don't want to outstay my welcome."

"But you were saying only yesterday that you were starting to like it here."

He chuckled. "I meant here, as in outside of prison walls."

"Oh," Jesse said nodding. "You want to go check on

71

Sara?"

Damon nodded.

It was strange; in the short time he'd got to know Jesse, they'd formed a friendship. It wasn't deep the way it was with Cole but they'd bonded over the small details of life. It was hard not to after their long journey out of New York and time inside the shelter. Even Maggie had started to warm up to him.

"Are you coming back?" Maggie asked.

"Not sure right now," Damon looked toward Elliot who was now looking over. "I just need a ride. It'll only take twenty minutes to get there."

"Well you might want to add an extra twenty on that if the roads are anything like this town. I felt like a pinball working my way around stalled vehicles. Lucky this thing is old," Jesse said giving one of the tires another kick. Damon shifted his weight feeling slightly uncomfortable at the thought that Elliot had told Rayna. She'd glanced at him and then said something before Elliot made his way over.

"You heading out?"

Jesse thumbed over his shoulder. "Yeah, gonna take him back."

Elliot nodded, his eyes darting between them. "About what I said, Damon."

"It's alright, I understand."

"No, you had no way of knowing this was going to happen." He cleared his throat. "Look, if things don't work out in Keene, you're welcome here. We certainly could use the extra help."

"I appreciate that."

"Right, well you should head out. Make sure you've got enough ammo," Elliot said to Jesse. Damon walked over and extended his hand, Elliot shook it.

"Thanks for everything."

It was awkward. How do you thank the man whose wife was nearly killed by the cousin of a close friend? Damon cut it short and hopped into the truck as Jesse slipped behind the wheel. He fired up the engine and Maggie came around.

"You coming too?" Damon asked.

"Yeah, someone's got to look out for him," she said, grinning at Jesse as she settled in for the trip. She reached into the glove compartment and pulled out a Glock and loaded a fresh magazine into it. Elliot watched them as they reversed out and then disappeared around the corner. After veering on to NY-72 E and leaving Lake Placid behind, Damon updated the two of them on his conversation with Elliot, just in case he decided not to return. There were two sides to every story, and he still wasn't sure Elliot understood his position. Their response was slightly different to Elliot's. Of course they had no emotional connection to his family or anyone in the neighborhood. Maggie just told him not to worry about it. What was done was done. Jesse remained quiet then blurted out a comment that didn't even seem to make sense.

"I killed two people this morning."

Both Damon and Maggie looked at him. He was gripping the wheel tight, his knuckles turning pale.

"And…?" Damon asked.

He kept his eyes fixed on the road. "We're living under different circumstances now. Who's to say Elliot's neighbors hadn't done something awful to someone else in town? I mean, it might not have been Magnus, right?"

"Possible," Damon muttered.

"For all we know that Scout could have belonged to the same person who gutted the chief."

"What's your point, Jesse?" Maggie asked.

"I'm just saying that everyone is doing what they can to survive, and if that means killing someone else," he shrugged. "Then so be it."

Damon snorted. "That's cold, even coming from you."

Even Maggie seemed amused by that.

"What?" Jesse asked. "I'm just saying. I don't think it's right what those two men were trying to do with Rayna but flip the coin over and see it from their point of view. Desperation can drive a man to do crazy things."

Neither he nor Maggie replied to that. They drove in silence for the rest of the journey. Damon mulled over the events of the morning but his thoughts were never far from the conversation he would have with Cole. If he was still alive, Damon expected him to have his fingers on the pulse in Keene — he wasn't the kind of man who would stand back and wait for the government to fix things, neither would he follow another. And if he was behind the deaths in Lake Placid, he'd want answers and that would only lead to more trouble. Sure, he could lie but if Magnus had spotted him or found out from the two people he'd killed that those he was with had been responsible for his cousin's death — things were about to get ugly.

Chapter 5

Foster Goodman had his reasons for killing Chief Wayland. The two of them hadn't seen eye to eye since the death of his son. Two years earlier his nineteen-year-old had died in a motorcycle collision in the north end of town. According to witnesses, not only had the driver of the SUV that hit him made an unsafe turn, but they were also intoxicated and had changed seats with the passenger. Though charges were brought against them, they were never convicted of vehicular manslaughter. In fact, they walked away with nothing more than a slap on the wrist and a license suspension. The driver of that SUV was the chief's wife.

Foster knew Wayland had covered it up and abused his power as chief because after it came to light that several officers in the department had brought forth allegations against him for violating town policies, procedures and general orders. This led to an investigation by internal affairs and for a brief while there was even talk of firing him due to employee intimidation, untruthfulness and multiple violations.

Except it never happened because the shit hit the fan.

All Foster wanted him to do was to confess that he had covered it up.

If he'd just admitted it, he might have still been alive. Except that wasn't the chief's way. He couldn't admit wrongdoing even though society was collapsing around them and there was very little chance he would ever operate in the same capacity as he had before.

As Foster sat there staring out over Mirror Lake, smoking a cigarette while two of his men sorted through the charred remains of another fire, his thoughts drifted back to that night — eight days after the lights had gone out.

Hunkered down in his house that night, the power outage had given him a lot of time to think. Too much time. After the death of his son and seeing his killer get away with manslaughter, he'd thrown himself into his work to keep his mind occupied. He thought if he could just stay busy, maybe, just maybe he wouldn't fall apart. The grief and stress of losing his only child had nearly cost him his marriage. His wife had become a shell of a person, never leaving the home and barely able to crawl out of bed in the morning. The only reason he'd been able to cope was because his work forced him to be out of the home, however, that all changed with the EMP. Now he had to face the very thing that he'd been ignoring and numbing with alcohol. Eventually he reached his breaking point.

By day eight the sound of violence echoed through the neighborhood. The constant sound of distant gunfire gave him an idea. Perhaps it was the alcohol lowering his inhibitions, or seeing his wife struggling to hold on to a reason to live, but when he left that night for Wayland's home with a .45 tucked into his waistband he had no intention of killing him.

When he arrived outside his home, he knocked on the door but got no answer.

He went over to the window and called out to him,

hoping he would hear but there was no response. Now he could have walked away. He'd had enough time to think about it on the way over, but he took Wayland's lack of response as another attempt to avoid admitting guilt. Something broke inside of him outside that home that night. He wasn't thinking right but then neither were those on the streets, lighting fires, looting stores and beating people for a loaf of bread.

Foster went around the back of the house, found the largest rock in his yard and used it to break the glass on the rear door. He reached in and unlocked it, and as soon as he entered he found himself staring down a Beretta.

"Back out, right now!" Chief Wayland said.

He backed up. "I just want to talk."

"You know I could arrest you?"

He chuckled. "Maybe you should go tell that to your neighbors who are breaking into the local convenience store across the street."

"Get out."

He put his hands up. "I just want to show you

something."

Foster slowly reached into his jacket.

"Don't do it."

"It's just a photograph." He pulled back the jacket so he could see there was nothing there except the picture. He pulled out the five-by-eight color photograph taken of his son weeks before his death and held it out. "He was just nineteen years old."

The photo was of him and his son in front of a new Kawasaki Ninja H2 Carbon. He'd wanted a brand-new bike since he was a kid.

"I know what he looked like."

Foster shook his head. "No, you don't."

Wayland wouldn't look at it. Instead he stayed focused on Foster.

"You know he was studying to become an engineer. He had these high hopes of doing something big with his life and that all changed that night your wife drove into him."

"She wasn't driving."

"BULLSHIT!" he bellowed, his hands shaking ever so

slightly.

"What do you want, Foster?"

"For you to acknowledge that you covered it up."

He shook his head and narrowed his eyes. "This is not the time or the place to have this discussion. Now I advise you..."

"To what? Huh? You going to shoot me, Wayland, and cover that up as well?"

He jabbed his handgun forward. "You're the one who broke into my house."

Foster slipped the photo back inside his pocket and kept his hands out. He continued staring at him even as he told him again to leave. He wasn't going anywhere, not until he got answers. He just needed him to lower the gun.

That's when the tears began to roll. Foster didn't need to fake them as they'd been building for years. He'd bottled up his emotions and pushed aside his hatred because that's what he was meant to do. That's what society had taught him to do. He wasn't supposed to grieve for years. No. Take a few months off. Go see a grief counselor. Find ways to deal with it and then come back and leave all that shit at home. But that hadn't worked. How could it when his son was lying in a grave and the one responsible wasn't behind bars? He'd come so close to seeing Wayland terminated from his position. And though it wouldn't have brought back his kid, it would have at least given him some satisfaction. It would have brought into question every incident that he'd ever been involved in, including the collision.

Slowly but surely Chief Wayland lowered his gun.

"C'mon, don't do that. Don't cry," he said. "Look… I'll get you a drink. We'll talk."

He backed up still not taking his eyes off Foster and pulled open a small cabinet. Inside were multiple bottles of liquor. He placed the gun down and filled two glasses with three fingers of bourbon, then brought one over and handed it to him.

"It's getting bad out there, isn't it?" Wayland asked.

Foster nodded. He listened to him drone on about the North Koreans and how nothing in life was truly black and white. There were gray areas — legal hoops that those in authority had to jump through and that's why things got dragged out. He was trying to justify his actions in some roundabout way but it was doing little to change Foster's mind. When Wayland's gaze turned away, he looked at how close that gun was and was thinking about how quickly he could pull his own.

"And that's why we'll be lucky if we see this country bounce back."

"Did you do it?" Foster asked gazing down into his drink, swirling it around in his hand. "That's all I want to know. Did you do it?" He didn't need to spell it out again, he was fully aware of what he was asking him to admit. He assumed under the circumstances there was nothing to hold him back from confessing.

"For what it's worth, Foster, I'm sorry for what happened. I'm not even with Lucy anymore. Our marriage broke apart seven months ago. And no, it had nothing to do with the media attention or even the accusations being thrown at me. Our marriage had been on shaky ground for some time."

Foster couldn't believe it. That's all he cared about — not

what he had done to others, to those in the department or even those he'd let slip through the justice system because of tainted evidence, or false reports — no, it was always someone else's fault.

"So did you do it?" Foster asked again.

"What do you think?"

He nodded. The man couldn't even admit to it. Foster didn't want to resort to violence but with every second that passed he could feel himself losing his grip. Wayland downed his drink. "I could use another, what about you?"

Foster hadn't touched his. He shook his head and Wayland turned and began unscrewing the top. The sound of metal against glass and his words mixed together like nails going down a chalkboard. He couldn't bear it anymore.

"Shut up," he said under his breath, so quiet that Wayland didn't hear him. Foster pulled up his shirt and clasped the grip of his Glock and pulled it from his waistband.

"Shut up!" he said now in a tone that was loud enough that he heard him.

"What?" he said turning around to find the Glock aimed at him. Wayland's hand started to shake; his eyes darted to his service weapon on the counter.

"Don't do it," he muttered under his breath. One second, then another passed and then Wayland dropped the glass he was holding and lunged for the gun. He had no chance. Foster squeezed the trigger, and it let out a pop, the round struck him in the chest. He stumbled back against the sofa and then slid down, dropping to the ground. He gripped his chest and opened his mouth as he tried to force words out.

"Get. An. Ambulance."

Foster walked over and loomed over him. With his free hand, he reached into his jacket and pulled out the photo of his son. "David Edward Goodman. Say his name."

Wayland's breathing got even more rapid as panic sank in.

"Say his name!" Foster yelled shoving the photo against the side of his face, then backhanding him with the gun.

"David Edward Goodman," Wayland blurted out.

"Now admit you covered it up. Say it."

"I…"

Perhaps he might have said it but he was now struggling to breathe.

"SAY IT!" Foster yelled.

His mouth opened, and he then he got this glazed look in his eyes as if the real person behind the meat suit was leaving.

"No, no, no. You say it now. Admit you covered up for your wife!"

His breathing became shallow and then he was gone.

"NO!" Foster yelled loudly. He got up and kicked the TV, smashing it against the wall. He went over to the sofa and pulled it down. He upended a chair and drove his foot through a glass panel that divided the living room from the hallway. Over the course of the next five minutes he unleashed his anger by going from one room to the next and smashing everything in sight. By the time he was done, it looked like someone had ransacked the home. Papers littered the ground, glass crunched beneath his boots, and ornaments were shattered.

He dropped to his knees and wept loudly, releasing all the

pent-up frustration, anger and heartache he'd buried. When he was done, he gazed at the mess and the body of Chief Wayland. That's when the shock set in. What had he done? His head shook ever so slightly as he tried to comprehend having taken a life. In the heat of the moment he didn't think about what he would feel after. Panic slowly started to creep up his chest, filling him with a deep sense of dread. Who had heard the gunshot? Was someone coming? He darted out the back door and peered into the darkness. No one was there. No one was coming. The occasional sound of gunfire echoing in the town gave him a smidgen of peace. It didn't last. He reentered the home and hurried over to where a bottle of bourbon lay. He unscrewed the top and chugged it back, wiped his lips with the back of his sleeve and looked down. The cogs in his mind started turning. He needed to make this look like a group of people had broken in and robbed him. People with a hatred for the police. Someone who didn't just want him dead, they wanted him to suffer. In the next few minutes his mind went into autopilot. He placed the bottle on the ground and went over to Wayland's lifeless body and took a firm grip on his wrists and dragged him out from underneath the sofa. He lugged his corpse into the kitchen and hauled him up onto the table. Next he tore open his shirt and gazed at the wound in his chest. He paced back and forth for a few minutes wondering if he should cut out the bullet. Even after all he'd been through, his mind was still processing it all as if a medical examiner was going to look him over — when the truth was no one was likely to touch his body.

Foster retrieved a large kitchen knife from a drawer and in a final act of bitter hatred he cut into his body, slicing him from sternum to abdomen. By the time he was done tearing at his flesh, his hands were covered in blood. Had he lost his mind? His hands began shaking, his eyes widened as he stepped back taking in the sight of the man he'd just brutalized.

He wiped his face with the back of his sleeve and could smell the iron.

What had he done? He couldn't even begin to comprehend the gravity of the situation. It wasn't meant to go this way. He was just meant to admit to it. Wasn't he?

He took several steps back, distancing himself from the macabre sight.

For over two years he'd thought about this moment, played out what he wanted to say and do and when it came down to it, he didn't even feel any better for it.

Foster dropped the knife and picked up his Glock off the counter and took one last glance at the body before bolting out the back door.

Chapter 6

Black smoke swirled over pines and into the gray sky as they finished the final leg of the journey. Sara Cooper lived on Bartlett Road in the north part of Keene. It was nestled between 2,300 acres of Sentinel Range Wilderness and the gushing waters of Phelps Brook. In the distance were the snowcapped peaks of Sentinel and Pitchoff Mountains. A moderate amount of snow had fallen over the past few days covering the wild and rugged terrain.

Damon instructed Jesse to give it some more gas.

Her father had purchased a large lot of vacant land along with a property that dated back to the 1960s. It was originally used as a summer camp but had fallen into disrepair and instead of abandoning it; the owners auctioned it off. He'd lucked out and snapped it up for a ridiculously low price, then renovated and built a gorgeous log home with four bedrooms.

For a time, he and Sara lived together but after he

ended up in Rikers, she lost her job. Of course, she'd told him she'd moved back in with her parents. It was easier that way.

Damon asked how she lost the job and although she said the restaurant couldn't afford to keep paying her salary, he knew that wasn't the reason. The trouble was with people yapping. Small towns were notorious for it, and with less than 1,100 people, rumors traveled fast, and bad reputation even faster. She wouldn't say it but her connection to Damon hadn't worked in her favor.

He was hoping to change that when he returned. There wasn't a day that went by that he hadn't thought of how he could turn it all around. He knew that if he got out, he had to distance himself from Cole, from the town, from anything that would come between them. But that presented challenges of its own. Her old man had always been against her moving away. She came from a large family, a religious one that believed in gathering every Sunday, meeting for family dinners once a month and sticking close so they could help each other out. He had no problem with that as he was born and raised in Keene and fully expected to die there. Except living there only worked if a person could find work, and there wasn't much of that going around. That's why they went into business for themselves. Cole knew his way around an engine as well as any trained mechanic, Devin had bodywork skills, and well, he had connections. Sawyer, Magnus and Tyron came into the picture later when Cole started looking at ways of supplementing their income through other means.

Sara on the other hand should have been the one to leave town. She had the grades, the charisma and drive that could have taken her places, but she listened to her old man — bought into his fear-based ideas. It was such a waste. Damon had told her that if she wanted a life, she needed to break away from them but she couldn't do it.

As they got closer to the turnoff, his mind churned over their last conversation on the phone. Sara had told him she didn't want to see him after he got out. She said it was best they cut ties with one another as it was doing neither of them any good.

He might have believed her had it been the first time she'd said something like that but it wasn't. Damon wasn't lying when he told Elliot his relationship with her had been on and off for years. He'd met her in high school and even though they went on to date other people, they got back together in their early twenties. When it was good, he could do no wrong, but once he went into business with Cole, that's when the arguments started.

Her parents hated Cole and anyone who associated with him.

It didn't matter that Damon got along with her parents or that they knew his livelihood depended on the business. They'd already made up their mind and there was no changing that.

The truck tore into the lot outside the two-car garage. The home was just over two thousand square feet, with an incredible landscaped yard, and a recent extension they'd added onto the back. It was this area that was up in flames.

Damon didn't hesitate; he pulled his Glock and pushed out of the truck before it even came to a stop. He dashed toward the front door which was wide open, and ran into the smoke-filled home keeping an arm over his face.

"Sara!"

There was no answer.

He pressed on even as he heard Jesse calling his name from behind. All his senses were on high alert as he darted upstairs to a spacious loft area, which had been converted into a master bedroom with a walk-out balcony for Sara. He coughed hard and squinted as he scanned the room. No sign of her. He bumped into Jesse on the way down.

"Damon, it's too dangerous."

"She's got to be here."

With every step forward it was getting harder to breathe. Snot trickled from his nose, and his eyes stung as he broke into a coughing fit. He moved into the back room of the house and tried to make out where the fire had started. Flames licked up the curtains, consuming everything in its path. He dropped to his knees and under the cloud of smoke he saw them.

Bob and Shirley were on the ground. He clawed forward even as Jesse protested. "This place is gonna collapse. Damon!"

He had to know.

His mind was in turmoil.

The air was thick with smoke making it almost impossible to see and even harder to breathe. He'd only made it a few more feet when a huge section from the rear of the home collapsed in. Massive blackened logs rained down crushing her parents.

A hand clamped on to the back of his jacket and the next thing he knew he was being dragged back across the hardwood floor.

"Get off," he yelled trying to break free from his grasp.

Jesse didn't reply until he'd hauled him out of the raging inferno.

The wood home crackled as it burned, and large pieces

of ash floated away on the breeze.

Outside Jesse released him and he broke into a coughing fit. Damon looked back at the house that was now fully engulfed. He staggered a little. His eyes burned from the heat.

"What the hell were you playing at, running in there? You wanna die?"

"She could be in there."

"If she is, she's dead."

"You don't know that," he shot back.

Maggie placed a hand on his shoulder and he shook it off and walked around the surrounding property. Black ash drifted to the ground, standing out against the brightness of white snow. Horrified and full of questions, Damon crouched and brought a hand to his smoke-covered face. As he looked on helplessly, he was at a loss for words. How did it start? Was it an accident or done on purpose? He'd seen many homes around Lake Placid set on fire. No one gave a damn now. If the power grid going out wasn't bad enough, now they had this shit to deal with.

"Damon!" He turned to see Jesse beckoning him. "You need to see this."

He got up and hurried down, following the driveway around to where Bob kept his boats. There on the side of his storage unit, sprayed in white paint were the words: *Damon! Baxter Mountain Tavern.*

* * *

Cole hurled a barstool across the room and it clattered on the ceramic floor.

"You did what?"

"Oh don't blame him," Magnus said. "Things got out of hand, the old man went for his rifle. If they had just done what we said, both of them would be alive."

"And if you had just done what I said, we wouldn't be dealing with this now. I told you no one gets hurt. What part of that didn't you understand?"

"I brought you Sara, didn't I?"

"Yeah, and you killed her parents."

"And burned down the house," Tyron added, shaking

his head.

"You fucking idiot! Do you even know what you've done?"

Magnus snorted. "I don't have to put up with this shit."

"No, you don't. The door is there if you want to walk," Cole said straightening up to him. He knew he was just venting hot air. He had nowhere to go. No family except them. Cole glanced over to Sara who was cowering in the corner of the room. He never had this in mind when he told them to go and collect her. All he wanted was a little leverage for when Damon showed up. He knew he would eventually arrive. Whether it was today or a week from now. There was no telling what he would do. Not that he was concerned, but he wanted an ace in his back pocket. Sara would have been that. But not now. This sent the wrong message.

"Why did you set the place on fire?" Cole asked. Magnus stared back at him and Cole just threw up a hand. "Actually, don't bother telling me. I don't want to know."

Devin and Tyron sat at the bar drinking cold beers after having been out for the past two hours trying to recruit others. They'd returned without even one person. It was unbelievable.

"And what about you two?"

Tyron shrugged. "It's bad out there, Cole. We had guns shoved in our faces; others wouldn't come to their doors. Like I told you, people don't trust anyone right now. Even if you were to roll up with a cooked chicken on the end of a stick, they probably wouldn't take it."

Cole shifted from one foot to the next shaking his head. A group of five wasn't enough. If they were going to take control of this town and ride out this shitstorm, they were going to need a new incentive.

"I keep telling you, you're going about this the wrong way," Magnus said while he sat on the sofa in front of a roaring log fire. He tossed in pistachio shells. "But no one wants to hear me."

Cole walked around the sofa and gestured. "Go on

then. Let's hear it."

"Oh, now you do?"

"Magnus."

"Alright. Tyron is right. People are too damn nervous right now to open their doors even if you genuinely are offering them a good thing. The only way to get them to listen is by force. Now I know you don't want to escalate to that, but we've tried your way. How about we try mine?"

"If I try yours, there will be no town left as it'll be burnt to the ground," Cole bellowed.

"Suit yourself," he said putting his feet up on a small coffee table and tossing another shell into the fire. Sawyer kept an eye on Sara to make sure she didn't bolt.

"What about you, Devin? What do you think?"

Although Devin tended to be quiet, and rarely gave his input, Cole trusted him. He hadn't yet led him down the wrong path and if whatever they were going to build here was to work, he needed to hear from others. It couldn't just be him. This wasn't a dictatorship.

He turned on his stool with a beer in hand. He ran his other hand over his goatee and shifted up his round John Lennon-style glasses into his mousy hair.

"You remember that guy who was dealing here in town before we got started?"

Cole nodded.

"He became our best distributor. I'm just saying."

He knew what Devin was getting at. Back when they first got into dealing drugs, most of the addicts and social indulgers already had a go-to guy named Ricky Jones. The guy had made a name for himself not only for being able to get anything, he'd also made it clear that this was his territory and no one else was dealing unless he got a cut of the profits.

His cut? Seventy-five percent.

Yeah. That didn't fly, but he did, straight off a ten-foot high deck.

He broke an arm and a rib in the fall, and Cole then rearranged his face and sent him a clear message — if he wanted to keep the rest of his bones intact he would either get the fuck out of Keene or operate as a distributor for him. Of course he opted to remain and take a measly percentage. Right up until the shit hit the fan, he was one of Cole's best dealers. He'd already earned the trust that money couldn't buy and in these parts that meant a lot. Nervous people didn't deal with those they didn't trust even if they dangled coke in front of their nose.

"So who then?" Cole asked.

"You need someone who has influence, who works in a place of power, someone who has earned the respect of residents. It might not be here, Cole, but if not here maybe try Lake Placid. Maybe Damon would know," Devin said.

"Right, use him to find out." He shook his head. "It's a little too late for that now you've killed his girl's parents and burnt their fucking house down!" he said glaring at Magnus.

Sawyer piped up. "What Devin said might work once we are established and are trying to edge into another town but until then we might have to give Magnus' way a try."

"Yeah, and what if they turn on us?" Tyron asked.

"They won't!" Magnus said. "Do you see her turning on us?"

"She doesn't have a gun in her hand, dick head. Eventually we are going to need to arm them. You want to arm someone who you have doubts about? People aren't going to follow us just because we stick a gun in their face. That's called wishful thinking. Make-believe. They'll turn the first chance they get," Cole said. "No, I say we try what Devin said. It takes just a small rudder to steer a boat. It's easier to control one man than to try and control a group. So I want you all to come up with some names. Put the feelers out, find out who was running the show in Keene before all of this happened."

"And Damon?" Magnus asked.

Cole snorted. "Leave him to me."

Sawyer pulled back the blinds that covered the main window. "Good. Because he's just arrived."

Chapter 7

Damon tucked his gun into the back of his waistband and readied himself for the worst. The truck rumbled outside the low-slung tavern. The roof was covered with a thin layer of snow. To the left of it was a two-car garage, and the entire lot was framed by rolling hills. The first thing he noticed as they pulled in was the sky blue 1979 Scout with the white stripe.

"Wait here," Damon said eyeing the windows that were covered by blinds. He saw someone peeking out. He tilted his head from side to side making a cracking sound.

"You're not going in there alone," Jesse said.

"This is between me and him."

"Yeah? And what happens if it goes south?"

"Then you get the hell out of here."

Maggie reached over. "Reconsider, Damon. You don't have to go in there."

"Yes, I do. I'll be okay." He gave a strained smile and

pushed out of the vehicle. He had no idea what the outcome would be but driving away wasn't an option. This had been a long time coming. There were two doors at the front of the cream clapboard structure with a green roof. He glanced at a faded American flag flapping in the breeze before he ventured in.

"There he is!" Cole said loudly with his arms out. "The prodigal son returns."

"Where is she, Cole?"

He snorted. "What, no hug for an old friend? Come, have a drink with me. We've got the whole place to ourselves." He studied him and remained where he was. Cole shook his head. "Oh God, Damon, she's fine. I wouldn't touch a hair on her head."

"So why did you murder her parents then?"

He got a pinched expression on his face. "That wasn't me. I'll give you three guesses who that was." He walked over to the bar where there were already two shot glasses on the counter. Damon took in his surroundings. Sawyer already had a firm grip on his handgun and was sitting at a table. Tyron was leaning up against the fireplace, his hand resting on his holster while Devin was keeping tabs on their truck outside. Cole began pouring bourbon into two clear glasses. He motioned with his head. "Come on. Have a drink. She's fine. You'll see her in a moment. I promise. This whole thing has been a big misunderstanding." He picked up a drink and held it out for him. Now Damon knew Cole well enough to know that despite his numerous downfalls, he was a fairly levelheaded guy. He wasn't rash like Magnus or Sawyer and for that reason alone he ambled over to the bar and took the glass from him. He waited until Cole knocked his back before he downed his. Cole got this big grin on his face and leaned in and hugged him.

"Man, it's good to see you. Really."

"So good that you couldn't take the time to come and pick me up?"

"Right... about that. Something came up and by the time I was available, the power had gone down."

"Convenient."

He was lying, but that was in the past now. All that matter was ensuring Sara remained safe and the best way to do that was to keep his cool and stay calm. Cole poured out another two drinks and then offered him a cigarette. He took it and Cole lit it with a cheap BIC lighter. Damon inhaled and did another scan of the room. Where was Magnus? Cole hopped onto a stool and scrutinized him.

"So how was New York?"

Damon hesitated before responding. "What are we doing here, Cole?"

"Having a conversation between two friends. We're still friends, aren't we?"

Damon didn't bother responding to that. Instead he took a sip of the bourbon, eyeing him over the rim. It burned the back of his throat but was slowly putting him at ease, which was exactly what Cole wanted.

"It was jail, what do you expect?"

He leaned against the bar. "You know, Tyron had you pegged as someone who was going to rat us out, isn't that right?"

Tyron glanced at him then looked away. They'd never really trusted each other. Their animosity for one another stemmed from the fact that Cole would always go to Damon or Devin for advice even though he'd known him since high school.

"But like I told them. That's not you. That's not Damon." He wagged his finger and smirked. "See, cause I know you're a stand-up guy."

He looked as if he wanted Damon to respond but he didn't. In the eight months he was inside Rikers, he'd thought about the conversation he'd have with Cole once he got out — the questions he'd ask, the accusations he'd make, but all those had fallen by the wayside in light of the situation. Cole continued to direct the conversation.

"So how did you get home?"

"I had my means."

Cole nodded. "Had a little help, you mean?" He looked over to Sawyer. "Those two in the truck outside, they from Lake Placid?"

Damon gave a nod.

He laughed. "Well why didn't you invite them in?"

"Look, where is Sara?" Damon said placing down his empty glass and starting to get agitated by the delay.

"I told you. She's safe and you'll see her in a minute. Now answer the question."

Damon's eyes bounced between him and Sawyer. He felt a single trickle of sweat roll down his back. It was uncomfortably warm inside. The logs in the fireplace crackled and static tension lingered in the air.

"I met them in New York."

"When did you get back?"

"Around two weeks ago."

He snorted and put his drink down. "You've been in our neck of the woods for two weeks and you didn't take the time to come by? Now I've got to say that's odd. That's odd, isn't it, Sawyer?"

"Yep!" he replied keeping his hand lightly against the gun laying on the table in front of him. He could sense the atmosphere in the room changing, like the shifting of wind. Damon figured it was best to explain.

"The country has suffered an EMP."

"Well no shit, Einstein!" Cole replied as his mouth wormed into a smile. "You got word on how it happened?"

"The guy I was traveling with believes it was a nuke. North Koreans."

Cole turned in his seat to face Devin. "You were right. I never trusted those little bastards. But you know what, Damon," he said turning back to him, "it proves a point. You don't need to be as big as Russia to bring a nation to its knees, you've just got to bide your time and wait for the right moment to strike. You see, everyone overlooks the little guy. They all think he can't be a problem. He doesn't have the means to cause trouble, and… even if he does, we'd see it coming." Damon had a sense he wasn't just speaking about the attack but himself. "But that's why you should never underestimate what a small group of people can do. Isn't that right, Devin?"

"I would say so."

Cole breathed in deeply. "It's good to have you back, Damon. Real nice. Ain't it, boys?" They all agreed keeping their gaze firmly fixed on him.

Damon cleared his throat. "Anyway. I figured it was safer to stay put for a couple of weeks and then head here."

"So this guy, the one who told you about the nuke. Is he out there?"

"Nope."

"So he stayed behind?"

He gave a nod.

"Um. And how many others are there?"

"Look, does it matter? Just bring out Sara and let's get this shit over with."

Cole rapped the bar with his knuckles and tucked his tongue against the edge of his cheek. "You in a hurry, Damon? I thought Keene was home?"

He didn't reply and just looked at him knowing full well that he wasn't going to let him walk out of there with Sara.

"It is but I've got to ask myself. Why is a guy who calls himself my friend holding my girlfriend hostage after killing her parents and burning their home down?"

Cole cleared his throat. "Magnus, bring her out here."

There was a commotion in the back room and farther down the bar Magnus came into view holding Sara by the arm.

"Damon."

Her eyes were swollen from crying, and she had a red mark on the side of her face.

"Sara!" Damon said stepping forward to approach. Cole put out his hand and placed it against Damon's chest. "Whoa. Slow down. There will be plenty of time for that reunion but right now we have things to discuss."

"Let her go, Cole."

He chuckled. "Don't act like that."

"Like what?"

"Like everyone else out there. Fearful. You've got nothing to fear. You're among friends."

"Then release her."

"I will but we have a little problem and an opportunity to discuss."

He picked up his glass and the bottle of bourbon. "Come on. Let's sit over by the fire."

Damon pointed at Magnus. "If you've laid a hand on her. I swear."

"Calm down, Damon, they haven't touched her."

He guided him toward the fireplace. It was a small section of the bar area that had been designed to give the place a warm and welcoming atmosphere. On the few times Damon had been there he'd seen it used by those who'd finished their meal and wanted to have a drink.

* * *

Outside, Maggie was beginning to worry. Jesse had kept the truck running and had the gearstick in reverse and his foot on the brake, just in case all hell broke loose. He'd already planned the escape route.

"He's been in there too long. We should go find out what's happening," Maggie said.

"You heard what he said. We wait."

"And if they've killed him?"

"They're friends of his, Maggie. I hardly doubt they're going to flush years of friendship down the drain."

"Really?" she said shaking her head. "They let him take the fall for a drug deal and then killed his girlfriend's parents and set the home on fire? Um, yeah, those are some real good friends."

He glanced at her. "What do you expect me to do? I can see one of them looking out."

"I don't know, I just don't like the feel of this."

"Nor do I but until we hear gunfire we stay put."

* * *

Damon gazed into the fireplace. Flames licked up blackened brick. Cole had been explaining what they'd managed to establish since the lights had gone out. They had more than enough liquor and a chef who they brought in at night to cook them a meal, and enough ammo to ward off anyone who thought of taking what they had. Out of the one thousand residents, many had died or fled. They were still assessing the situation and trying to determine how many remained.

"And that's where you come into all of this. You see, we can go out there and drag a few people out of their homes and force them at gunpoint to assist us but that isn't going to get us anywhere, except an early grave once they have a gun in their hand. We need more people, Damon. That's the road to riding out this shit storm. We can hunt in the surrounding forests for food but that's hard work when there are only five of us. We can scavenge for fuel, ammo and supplies from surrounding towns but that's only going to get harder as others defend what they own." He took a deep breath, downed the rest of his drink and set it down. He pulled out his pack of cigarettes and rolled around a cigarette in front of his face. "I thought that food, bullets, water and creature comforts were the new commodities but that's not the truth. Trust and respect is," he said cutting him a glance. "If you have those the rest will come. And right now that's what we are looking at — ways to thrive not just survive this." He leaned forward in his chair and placed the cigarette between his lips and lit it. "And you're going to help us with that."

"I just want Sara and then I'm out of here."

Damon looked over to her and gritted his teeth.

"Where you gonna go?"

"Away from here."

"Lake Placid?"

"Maybe. Maybe somewhere else."

"And why would you do that? She's not even with you anymore. She did tell you that, right?" A bemused smile flickered on his face.

Damon kept his gaze on Sara. Cole turned in his seat. "Eight months changes people, Damon. Sara, tell him who you've been screwing since then. Go on."

"Enough, Cole," Damon said.

"Oh, I would have thought out of anyone you'd want to know who she's been spending time with." He looked back at Sara. "Liam Shaw, isn't that right, Sara?"

She didn't respond, her chin dropped. Damon fully aware that she might have been seeing someone while he was inside. He wouldn't fault her for that. Neither did it come as a surprise to him. They'd dated others between the times they'd been together. And he didn't expect her to wait for him. Pressure from her father probably factored into it. Liam Shaw was a clean-cut guy, someone that attended the same church as her. She'd probably been set up by her old man.

"Anyway before we get back to what I need you to do, there is a slight issue that must be resolved, and that's the death of Austin and Trent. You see, Magnus here is real torn up about it and while Trent was an asshole — no offense, Magnus — they would have come in real handy with building connections in Lake Placid. Now I'm down two men and out of pocket. I can't let that slide. So I figure with you being in Lake Placid for the past two weeks, you might be able to shed some light on what happened. So?"

"I don't know shit. If they're dead, they probably brought it on themselves."

"Well that's what I told Magnus but you know how he

is about kin."

"Can't help you." Damon got up and motioned with two fingers for Sara to come over to him. Magnus grabbed a hold of her arm.

"Sit down, Damon," Cole said in a stern voice.

"Let her go!"

"She's not going anywhere, and neither are you until we reach an understanding."

Magnus withdrew his sidearm and cocked the gun.

Damon couldn't believe these were the same people he'd left behind — friends he'd relied on, shared drinks with and gone out of his way to help. At one time they'd been a tight group. Now all he felt was animosity.

Damon looked down at Cole and balled his fist. If it wasn't for the fact that they were armed, he would have gone nuclear on them. It wouldn't have been the first time he'd had to fight five guys. That had become a regular way of life inside Rikers. It was rare that anyone got attacked by one guy. It might have started that way, but it always morphed into a group attack.

Chapter 8

When the call came over the two-way radio for assistance, Elliot couldn't ignore it. He'd spent the last hour erecting signs around his property in different spots in the forest and rolling out fencing with barbed wire. Some might have seen it as over the top and perhaps it was, but it was work that kept his mind occupied. In New York there was never a moment when he wasn't thinking about how to survive so this just felt like a natural extension of the past year. The only difference was small-town living was less distracting. City life kept him from spending too much time overanalyzing his issues or thinking about Rayna and the kids. Now he just wanted to take measures to ensure they stayed safe above and beyond the shelter.

"Elliot, come in," Gary said. Static crackled over his voice. He sounded like he was on the move.

Though he hadn't officially told him that he'd help

with town issues, Gary had taken it upon himself to assume he would pitch in. Two weeks ago they had a team of about ten officers. It was a small department, but it was enough to handle the general problems. That was before the power went out. It had only taken a couple of weeks for chaos to ensue and the town's infrastructure to buckle beneath the weight of the challenges. Garbage was no longer being hauled away so there had been an increase in wild animals rifling through dumpsters and black plastic bags on the streets. And that was just the beginning. With grocery stores being looted and resources running in short supply, it didn't take long before self-perseveration kicked in and fighting broke out. There were even rumors that neighbors had formed small groups that would work together to take what they wanted. Though most of the emergency services had remained operating, others had done what anyone in their right mind would do, and eventually left town so they could focus on saving their own ass.

That meant they were down several officers and those

that remained were pulling all manner of shifts. In many ways the community was forced to come together. Some were volunteering, stepping up to the plate to watch over the roads, while others offered protection to those still using the medical center, the town hall and Olympic Center. Elliot unclipped the radio from his belt and ambled back to the house.

"Yeah, I'm here, go ahead."

"We've got a problem. Officer Jackson was sent out to take over the shift at the Olympic Center and oversee the unloading of supplies into the back room when he ran into some trouble. He never arrived. A resident on West Valley Road said she saw four individuals dump a truck in the ditch near Fawn Ridge and take off on foot into the forest. I need you to swing over with the Jeep and meet me at the corner of Valley and Cummings Road as the rest of our vehicles are out."

"You think they're heading for the residential area?"

"Either that or they're camped out in the woodland. Either way I don't want to take any chances."

He let out a heavy sigh. "Yeah, I got it."

"And Elliot. Bring your rifle, and Kong as we might need his help, over."

It was to be expected people would start creating factions, splintering off into groups and taking any measure to survive. Elliot dropped the roll of barbed wire and gave a whistle. From the back of the house, Kong came bounding out followed by Evan.

"Evan, tell your mother I'm heading out to meet with Gary."

"Can I come?"

"Not this time."

"Why not? I'm old enough to help."

"Too dangerous, son. Besides, who's going to look after your mother?"

He got this proud look on his face and Elliot ruffled his hair. "Go on, inside, I'll be back later."

His son stared at him and he turned to walk away. That's when it dawned on Elliot what he'd said. *I'll be back later.* Those had been the same words he'd said to

Evan before he left for New York. Elliot clenched his jaw, ambled over to him and got down to his level. "You know I'm not going to leave you again, okay? You understand that?"

Evan nodded but whether he believed him or not was another thing entirely. It wasn't easy earning someone's trust; it was even harder to gain it back. He gave his son a hug and lingered in the embrace to reassure him that he meant it. His kids meant everything to him. He'd done a lot of things wrong in his life but having them was the best part of him. They represented everything that was right and good and untainted.

Evan jogged back to the house and Elliot went down into the bunker and put on a ballistic vest. He retrieved his rifle, palmed a mag into it and slung it over his shoulder. He scooped up a few more magazines and secured his handgun in his holster around his waist. Kong was waiting for him at the top of the ladder. "Hey boy, go get in the truck." That was all he needed to say and he sprinted around the house. By the time Elliot made it, he was waiting for him, panting with his tongue hanging out his mouth.

It was a quick seven-minute journey down Mirror Lake Drive, across Victor Herbert to reach the crossroads of Valley and Cummings. There were several homes nestled into the woodland. Gary was already there chatting with a resident. He'd brought along two locals, one was Richie Summers, a gas station attendant but an avid hunter, and the other was a woman in her late thirties. She had dark hair swept back and tucked through a baseball cap. The face was familiar but he couldn't place the name.

The Jeep rumbled as he stuck the gear into park. Gary broke away from the man he was chatting to and jogged over. He pointed toward the forest. "Apparently around twenty minutes ago they were seen lugging boxes of supplies through the forest. Jackson was still alive," he said. "You can park the Jeep in this gentleman's garage. I know him. It'll be safe there." Elliot swung the Jeep around and went up a short driveway and entered a vacant spot. The garage was as clean as a whistle. He hopped out and darted back over to the group as they headed toward the tree line.

"By the way this is Richie and Laura."

Elliot gave a nod.

"Heard good things about you," Laura said.

"Then you haven't lived long enough in this town," he replied as he pressed on ahead.

Gunfire echoed north of town. There was no telling if it was them or someone else. Tracking down those responsible for crime was getting harder by the day and with limited resources and manpower eventually they would have to realize it was too much to handle. Elliot glanced at Gary as they trudged into the thick snowy underbrush. Kong went ahead but stayed close. All it took was one whistle and he could get him to stop in his tracks. It didn't matter if he'd seen a rabbit; he'd been trained well.

"So did you have the talk with Ted?" Elliot asked, his eyes scanning the darkest parts of the forest. He'd brought the rifle off his back and chambered a round. He wouldn't think twice about killing anyone who tried to take his life but the others, he had his doubts about them.

"Yep, it didn't go too well. But that was to be expected."

"What are his thoughts on the current situation?"

"He wants me to deputize certain members of the community. Those he trusts."

"That might work."

"Or it might lead to trouble."

"I wouldn't worry about it. I don't think we'll get to that stage," Elliot said as he moved ahead.

"You know, Elliot, even in the 1800s they still had law and order."

He replied without looking, "Of course."

"Then why do you want to abandon what infrastructure we have in place?"

"Did it protect Rayna?" Elliot asked.

"You know as well as I do that we've been operating at a disadvantage. If I'd known they were in trouble, I would have been over there. You know damn well I would have," Gary shot back.

"So why didn't you respond to her call?"

The wind rustled the tree branches, and a chilly breeze brought the scent of pine.

"What?"

"Rayna said she tried getting through to you on the walkie-talkie."

"Um. Let me see. It was at the house with Jill and I was a little busy dealing with an angry mob that was demanding answers for what we were doing."

"And what were you doing?"

"Everything we could!" he shot back in an angry tone.

There was a moment of awkward silence, then a bird squawked overhead putting all of their nerves on edge. They stopped walking and took in their surroundings.

Gary bristled. "I'm not sure where you're going with this, Elliot, but we are doing the best we can under the circumstances."

"No one is paying you, Gary."

"And so that's the deciding factor, as to whether you help or not? C'mon, you can't believe that. If you did, you wouldn't be here now."

"You're a friend. I'm doing you a favor."

Gary frowned. "Yeah, right. So if it was anyone else asking, you would turn your back on them?"

He shook his head. "I'm just saying we need to pick our battles. And right now the biggest one we are facing is riding out this shit storm. The more time we spend out here chasing down ghosts, manning roads and protecting what little we have left is time we could use to ensure our loved ones don't end up on the end of a bullet."

Gary nodded. "I agree to an extent and I understand where you are coming from but the road out of this storm is by us working together as a community, not abandoning each other to fend for ourselves. That's a surefire way to end in disaster."

"Maybe. Maybe not."

He scoffed. "Talking to you is like speaking to a wall. No wonder Rayna struggled."

"What's that mean?"

"I'm just saying, you didn't make it easy for her."

"No, I mean, why does she matter to you?"

"Because we've been friends a long time, Elliot, and when you went away for a year, Jill and I were the ones she turned to. Did she tell you that?"

Rayna hadn't mentioned it since his return. Of course he figured that Gary and Jill would have helped out and that's why he'd been able to get through each day without worrying as much.

"She didn't say anything about that."

"Yeah, well maybe she didn't want to make you feel bad. But walking out on those kids… that was just—"

Elliot stopped walking and cut him off. "It is none of your damn business. Now I would advise you to tread carefully with what you say next. Because this…" He looked around. "This doesn't mean shit to me. I can walk out of here and not lose an ounce of sleep."

"Yeah, I believe you," Gary said walking on as Elliot stared at his back.

"And your point?"

He cast a glance over his shoulder. "It means you're good at walking away from uncomfortable situations."

Elliot chuckled. "Yeah, and you're uncomfortable walking into them."

"What are you suggesting?"

"I'm not suggesting anything. I'm calling a spade a spade. You didn't show up that night to help her because you were too damn scared. It's the reason you have three of us out here right now."

"Oh no you don't. You're not going to spin this around and pass the buck just because someone called you out on your own shit."

"Are you guys always like this?" Richie asked.

"Shut up!" both of them told him in unison. He tossed a hand up and pressed on down the trail that would lead to a wealthy section of Lake Placid. The Fawn Ridge area was known for having some of the most expensive homes in the town. Most of them sat back from Algonquin Drive, which snaked its way through the heart of the forest.

It was just a hunch that's where they were heading based on where Kong was leading them, but it would have been where Elliot would have gone if he was trying to stay out of sight. Most of the homes were about two miles away from the main stretch and were shrouded by forest and only accessible by two roads. One from the west called Sugar Run and Algonquin Drive from the north.

Elliot jogged ahead to catch up with Kong who had taken off at a rapid pace after sniffing the ground.

"Slow down, Elliot. They're armed," Gary said.

"So am I."

"I don't want you shooting anyone. We can deal with this peacefully."

He snorted and muttered under his breath. "Peacefully?" He was living in a pipe dream of a community that would watch each other's back and glossing over what was in front of him. It had to be the same for all the towns and cities in the country. Those who had food and supplies would be attacked first. Lake Placid was no different. Elliot stayed low raking his rifle ahead of him while keeping the pace with Kong who had slowed to a trot just a few feet from the clearing of a home. "What you got, boy?"

As he caught up with him and looked toward the home. One of the lower windows was smashed as if someone had broken in. He took a knee by a thick pine tree as he waited for the other three to catch up. When Gary arrived he was out of breath and panting.

"Did you not hear me?" he asked.

"What?" Elliot replied. He'd heard him but wasn't in the mood. He gestured with his head. "My guess is they're inside the home. How do you want to do this?"

"Now you listen." Gary shook his head. "Richie, Laura head around front. We'll take the rear. If you see them don't engage. I repeat don't engage. They are armed and have an officer. I don't want to lose him. I want to speak to them first."

"Roger that," Richie said veering off to the left with

Laura in his shadow.

"You want to tell me why you picked them?" Elliot asked.

"They volunteered."

"And you allowed them to tag along?"

"Is there a problem Elliot? They not up to your tactical standards?"

"I just don't want them to get hurt."

"Oh so now you care?"

"Whatever, man, let's do this."

Elliot ignored him and burst out of the tree line running at a crouch.

Chapter 9

Cole wouldn't take no for an answer. He was a stubborn sonofabitch.

"I can't help you, now let her go," Damon said.

"Listen to me, Damon." Cole leaned forward and gripped his arm. "I think you've underestimated what you've earned from these people. They trust you. If they didn't they would be gone by now." He looked over to Sawyer who confirmed Jesse and Maggie were still out there. "Now all I'm asking is for you to work with me here. You said yourself, this Elliot guy is friends with a cop. That's the kind of influence we need. Someone who the town is looking to for answers."

"I don't think you're listening," Damon replied. "It's not happening."

"It's simple. You don't even need to tell them anything. They're not going to bat an eye if a few items go missing, or another house is set on fire or a truck is stolen. You said yourself — all manner of shit is happening in town right now. They can't keep up with it. We're just going to speed up the process. We shake their confidence, and then present ourselves at their darkest hour offering accommodation, food and medical supplies. We'll enter into a trade agreement. Food for work. Medical supplies for loyalty. It's where everything is heading right now. They'll have no other choice." He leaned back and took a hard pull on his cigarette and blew the smoke out his nostrils. "We'll be painted in a good light and we'll have the foundations for building something great."

"Something great? Do you even hear yourself? You're out of your mind."

"No, I've never been clearer. We'll handle things here in Keene and make sure there are enough supplies ready. You'll handle getting the ball rolling in Lake Placid. It's a win-win situation. We're not harming anyone."

"You already have."

"That was a mistake, stop bringing it up," he said in a

rough voice.

Damon took a drag on his cigarette. "Okay. What if I agree? Do you have supplies in place now?"

"The wheels are in motion."

Damon laughed. "Cole, you are full of shit, you know that? You expect me to believe that no one is going to get harmed? Then how are you going to gather what you need to offer those in Lake Placid?"

"Leave that to me."

"No, come on. Tell me."

Cole squinted as smoke spiraled up into his eyes. He leaned forward and pulled the cigarette from his lips and blew it away. "The needs of the many outweigh the needs of the few."

"So you're going to kill a few people?"

"I didn't say that."

"You don't need to, it's obvious." Damon got up and beckoned for Sara. "Let's go."

"She's not going anywhere."

"You said you were going to let her go."

"And I will once you've done what I've asked."

"The last time I did that, I wound up in jail. It's not happening again."

Damon walked round the sofa heading toward Magnus.

"Magnus!" That was all Cole needed to say, and he raised the gun to the side of Sara's head. "Don't make this more difficult than it needs to be, Damon. We're friends."

"Friends don't do this," Damon shouted keeping his eyes on Magnus, as his hand slowly slipped around to reach for his gun. Before he could grasp it, Sawyer came up behind him and he heard the cock of a gun and felt the barrel touch the back of his head. Then, his own gun was removed from his waistband. Sawyer tossed it to Cole.

Cole sighed. "Man, I was really hoping to avoid this. I thought you were smarter than this, Damon. I thought we had something good going on and there you go ruining it." He took a deep breath. "It's not like it's complicated. I'm not asking for a lot. You need to survive. I need to survive. People out there need to survive. I'm trying to do a good thing here and you're fucking it up!" He tapped the barrel of the gun against his temple like a lunatic.

"A good thing? You're so deluded you can't even see it. People don't want to be controlled."

"Did I say anything about control?" Cole asked.

"Don't bullshit me. You know damn well that's what you have in mind. Tell me, Cole, what happens when people overstep the line, huh?"

A thick tension was building in the room.

"We'll deal with that when we get to it. Right now, we're not even close. I don't understand, Damon, why you're against this. Would you rather I forced people to help me?"

"Why do you need to have anyone help you? Why can't you be the one helping others without ties?"

"Shit." He ran a hand over his head and paced. "How many goddamn ways do I need to explain this for you to get it? I'm trying to help people. I want… to help people. Just like your friends out there. But there is a cost to doing business. Why the hell do you think we pay so much tax to the government? It's not personal. It's just business. I'm a businessman. And believe me, just because the world has gone to shit that doesn't mean anything has changed in how I conduct business. This is how I'm proposing to do it. I'm looking to get people hooked. Is that clear enough for you?"

"Oh it's clear," Damon shot back.

"Then work with me."

Damon knew Cole enough to realize that when he had his mind set on anything, nothing could sway him. And those who went against him suffered. Unless he agreed he wasn't walking out of there. Of course he wasn't gonna go along with Cole's asinine plan. After the shit he'd put him through? Hell, no! The very fact that he expected him to get onboard proved he wasn't all there in the head. But he wasn't going to let him know that.

Damon sighed, then nodded slowly. "Okay."

Cole's eyebrow arched. "Okay, you're onboard?"

"Like I had a choice."

"We always have choices, some work, some don't," Cole replied.

Cole turned and gave a nod for Magnus to release Sara. She ran forward, and he was about to hug her when she slapped him across the face.

He reached up and touched his cheek, which was now on fire. She'd always had one hell of a hook on her. "Holy shit, what was that for?"

Cole and the others burst out laughing. "Damn! I told you she's batshit crazy."

"For my parents." She lashed out again, and he grabbed her wrist.

"I didn't kill them."

"But you agreed with this asshole who did."

Damon held her tight and then slowly she pressed herself against him and sobbed. Cole chuckled as he walked back over to the bar and put the bottle back. "Now how about you invite your friends in? Introduce us.

We'll have supper. Sawyer, go get Pete."

"Now?"

"Yeah. Now!"

He trudged away and pushed out of the north exit door.

"I've got a good feeling about this, Damon. It's going to be like old times. Just like when we went into business together." He turned to Devin to see if he wanted steak. Magnus didn't take his eyes off Damon for even a second. He could see his Glock on the bar beside Cole as he'd laid it down.

"You think I can get my gun back?" Damon asked.

Cole diverted his gaze away from Devin. "Yeah, sure, later." He smiled. "Go call your friends in. Let's meet them."

"Okay." Damon nodded and headed toward the door with Sara.

"Oh and Sara darling, you take a seat over there. He's coming right back."

They were three-quarters of the way to the exit.

Damon scanned the room. Magnus was holding his piece down at his side. Devin didn't have his out and his own gun was within inches of Cole's grasp. He considered bolting but the odds of being shot were too high. Instead, he used the moment to his advantage. Damon kept hold of Sara's hand.

"You don't trust me, Cole?" Cole studied him, his fingers tapping out a rhythm on the bar. "Cause if you don't trust me what's to say that I'm going to do anything you say when I return to Lake Placid?"

He chuckled. "Alright. Alright. Go on then, you two love birds."

Damon squeezed her hand and tugged her toward the door. Once they were outside, and the door began to close, he could see Sawyer heading north on Highway 9 in the blue Scout. Without missing a beat he burst forward dashing for the truck holding Sara's hand. "Let's go," he yelled. Damon had just reached the passenger side and was about to get in when he heard — Pop. Pop.

The sound was unmistakable. He turned his head to

find Sara clutching her chest. Two rounds had punctured her back and gone straight through her. In that moment his world slowed. He heard return gunfire and Maggie yelling for him to get in. His eyes darted to the tavern just in time to see Magnus duck inside. He hauled Sara's limp body into the vehicle and Jesse smashed his foot against the accelerator and tore out of the lot under heavy fire from Magnus and Devin. The passenger side window shattered sending glass all over Maggie.

Sara was gasping, sucking air in rapidly.

"Stay with me," Damon said trailing fingers gloved in blood around the side of her face. Her eyes were glazing over and her body was heaving. Contrary to what the movies portrayed, people didn't always die immediately when struck by a bullet. It depended on distance, the type of bullet, the impact and the path it took inside. Still, even if the bullet hadn't hit an artery, they could still die from hemorrhagic shock.

* * *

Elliot shouldered the rifle and pushed forward through

the trees, moving with purpose and speed around the other edge. They didn't want anyone to look out and see footprints in the snow leading up to the side of the house. The wind was picking up, blowing snow in their faces like sharp needles. Kong stayed close, possibly sensing danger? Behind him Gary watched his six while Elliot scanned the windows of the custom-built Adirondack style home. *Who owned the place?* It was located in one of the most prestigious areas of Lake Placid. Only those with deep pockets could afford homes around there.

As they got closer, he heard voices and hurried over to the rear of the house and pressed his back against it.

"You know they're going to send the cops out looking for him."

"They'd have better luck finding a needle in a haystack. Now stop worrying."

"Do you trust him?"

"Of course I do. He's already delivered twice and without asking us to do anything."

With one hand gripping his AR-15 and the other

holding a firm grip on Kong, he waited, fully expecting to see them round the corner. A cigarette butt was flicked into the snow and then their voices grew distant. Elliot looked down.

"Stay here, Kong. Don't move."

Kong dropped, his thick fur protecting him from the cold. He would have taken him in the house but with glass on the ground and armed assailants he wasn't trained for that.

Gary tapped his shoulder to let him know it was time to move. He took a deep breath and stepped forward, pushing away the memories of Fallujah. It felt like he was reliving it again, clearing homes looking for insurgents. He climbed the eight steps to the deck taking two at a time and got real low and approached the closest window. He peered inside to where one guy was sitting at the kitchen table rolling a joint. Without saying any words, he motioned to Gary using hand signals to alert him to the presence of one suspect. Elliot crept underneath the window and shifted over to the next. The new view gave him a shot of the hallway, and a partial glimpse of the living room where he could just make out Officer Jackson sitting on a couch. A female crossed over and Elliot quickly pulled back.

He took another look, and this time saw a different guy with a Mohawk. On the back of his leather jacket were the words: Sex, Drugs and Rock and Roll. Below that was the peace symbol used in the nuclear disarmament campaign. He snorted. The irony wasn't wasted. He tossed up two fingers and then was just about to head for the rear door when they heard gunfire coming from the front of the house. The staccato of an assault rifle caused both of them to go on high alert.

"That better be someone else," Gary said suggesting that returning fire wasn't the answer. He was an idealist. The instincts he'd gained from being a Marine had been replaced when he signed up as a cop. The police taught communication then various degrees of enforcement and only resorting to use of weapons if they felt their life was in jeopardy. It was extremely effective in the normal world but this was a very different world now. Inside he could see two men alerting the others that they had company. It was now or never. He moved toward the door, and Gary pulled the screen door open. He swung his rifle behind him and withdrew his Glock for close quarter combat. Elliot cut the corner to make sure the coast was clear then moved in. A male suspect darted into the corridor and before he could fire off a round or even open his mouth, Elliot fired one in the chest, and another in the head sending him down. Gary veered off into the nearest room taking the right while he went left.

The woman let out a scream and darted out with a machete in hand. It narrowly missed his face as she cut the air in a wide arcing motion. With the precision of a laser, Gary fired a round, and it opened her skull. She collapsed just as the walls were peppered with rounds. Both Gary and Elliot hit the floor as the boom of a shotgun tore up the drywall and blew a hole through the adjoining door. Wood went flying, and the room filled with white dust from drywall.

A door at the front of the house swung open and the final two assailants rushed out unleashing a flurry of bullets at Laura and Richie. Elliot stumbled to his feet and hurried down the corridor, he pointed to Jackson who was lying on the ground with his hands zip tied. He stayed behind the wall near the front entrance as the gunfire continued. Looking toward the road he saw Richie on the ground, bleeding out, while Laura took out the legs of one of the kidnappers as he tried to make a dash for it.

The other lay near the front gate coughing and spluttering. In the short time it took for Elliot to make it over to him, he breathed his last. But his buddy, the one screaming in agony and clutching his leg in the middle of the road, was very much alive.

Chapter 10

Damon rested his forehead against Sara's as she took her last breath. He wiped away the blood that trickled from the corner of her mouth. Jesse glanced over. They were doing over 80 mph, trying to put as much distance as they could between the tavern and them. Damon's heart was pounding in his chest. It all happened so quickly. Too quickly.

Homes and trees whipped by in his peripheral vision.

"What now?" Jesse asked.

He got no response from either of them.

"Damon. What now?" he asked again hoping to snap him out of it.

He'd turned his head for just a second when the front windshield cracked and a bullet struck Maggie in the shoulder. The truck swerved, and he had trouble keeping the tires on the ground.

Damon looked out to see Sawyer standing in the

middle of the road. Behind him the blue Scout was positioned across the center line to prevent them from driving past. He had his rifle raised. Before Damon could tell Jesse what to do, there was another pop, then another and Jesse almost lost control of the vehicle. Their vehicle shot past Sawyer, smashing into the rear corner of the Scout. Metal crunched, sparks flew, and he fully expected them to wind up in the ditch. They didn't. They veered off the road, tore up the snow-covered shoulder and he managed to get back on the road leaving Sawyer taking a few more potshots at the truck. Damon looked back and saw him get on a radio. A plume of grit and dirt kicked up, and by the thumping sound, he knew a round had struck a tire.

"Maggie," Jesse yelled.

Maggie was clutching her left shoulder and screaming in pain. Her head tipped back, her mouth agape. Damon had to let Sara go so he could try and help Maggie. Meanwhile Jesse was becoming distracted, panicked and overwhelmed. They swerved as the one flat tire caused the vehicle to pull to one side.

"Focus on the road," Damon shouted.

"Which way?"

"What?"

"Which way do I go?"

In his panicked state he'd missed the turnoff for Lake Placid and was heading north on Highway 9. At the rate he was going they'd hit Jay Mountain Trailhead.

"Shit," Jesse said.

"What is it?"

He tapped the gas indicator. Damon glanced in his side mirror and saw that a round had struck the fuel line, now they were losing fuel by the second. This was not good. Not good at all. If that wasn't bad enough he caught sight of the blue Scout behind them in the distance.

"Give it more gas," Damon yelled looking over his shoulder.

"I'm giving it everything it's got."

As they followed the winding road, which cut through

the north part of upstate New York, the Adirondack high peaks loomed on either side, a dense woodland that fed into the Sentinel Wilderness. Damon glanced into the back of the truck at what they'd brought with them, it wasn't much but he had an idea.

"Pull off."

"What?"

"Pull off. This truck isn't going to get us far. We need to take cover in the woodland." He glanced back in his mirror and saw that Sawyer was getting closer. The fuel in the truck was nearly gone. In a matter of minutes it would be spluttering and stalled at the edge of the road, at least if they got off now they could increase the odds of survival.

"Do it now!" he bellowed. Jesse swerved on the hard shoulder, gravel and snow crunched beneath the tires. Damon was the first out. He reached into the back of the truck and pulled out a custom Ruger 22 rifle, it already had a magazine in. He chambered a round and brought it up while yelling orders to Jesse.

"Get Maggie out and into the forest. Now!"

He glanced at Sara's slumped-over body and clenched his jaw. He could feel rage welling up inside him. Jesse pushed out his side and ran around to help Maggie out. She was wincing in pain and groaning.

"Grab the rucksack in the back."

Damon had to give Elliot props for being prepared even if everyone else wasn't. He'd made a point to keep the vehicles fueled up at all times, and made sure that a few basics items were in a backpack, loaded in the truck just case they had to leave in a hurry. As Sawyer got closer, Damon squeezed off three rounds one after the other aiming for the windshield. He moved forward while Jesse and Maggie pitched sideways down a ditch heading for the wilderness. The beauty of a Ruger 22, one of the most popular rifles in the world, was that it was completely customizable. The magazine Elliot had put in this one held up to twenty-five rounds so Damon didn't hesitate to use every single one to bring down this asshole.

The blue Scout screeched to a halt and Sawyer

slammed into reverse as Damon kept him under steady gunfire and peppered the vehicle. He watched as Sawyer spun it around and took off at a high rate of speed leaving a plume of dust in its wake. Unlike Magnus he wasn't a psycho, just a blind follower of Cole. They all were. Manipulating people was his greatest strength. He led others around by enticing them with money, so it wasn't a surprise to think he would try to do the same now that money had no value. Commodities changed, people like him didn't.

Damon had fired nine shots before he stopped. He remained on the road for the next minute or two to make sure Sawyer didn't turn around before heading back to the truck. He glanced at the holes in the rear and the remaining fuel leaking to the ground. The thing was a write-off. Inside the cab he reached across and dragged Sara's dead body out and put her over one shoulder. She wasn't heavy at all. No more than a hundred and twenty pounds wet. He kicked the door closed and trudged down the incline and up the other side to join Jesse in the tree line. He could have left her there, but she deserved a proper burial even if it would be a shallow grave.

The afternoon sky had shifted, squeezing out what little blue remained and replacing it with nothing but a dreary and bleak gray. It did little to ease his mind. He ducked under a branch and pushed his way through the thick underbrush. The Sentinel Wilderness was a huge area that covered 2,300 acres and surrounded the towns of Keene, Jay, North Elba and Wilmington. The most noticeable attraction was the mountains, the snow-brushed Sentinel and Pitchoff, and the Kilburn, which was the highest peak at just below 4,000 feet. It was rugged terrain and easy to get lost in. It certainly wasn't for amateurs. It was full of ponds and wetlands and often used for hiking, camping, rock and ice climbing in the winter, fishing in the summer and hunting all year round.

"Where the hell are we going?" Jesse said. "We need to treat her wound."

"We will."

"When?"

"Once we've put some distance between us and the road. They'll be back and when they do I want to be ready."

"Back?" Jesse spat. "What happened back there?"

Damon didn't answer; instead he trudged on heading in a southwesterly direction. Twigs snapped beneath his boots and he stopped to adjust Sara's body. He planned to camp for the night, bury her and then in the morning loop around to Keene and drop in on an old friend. The sound of the Ausable River got closer as they threaded their way through the vast expanse of pine and fir trees. He knew this place well, so did Cole and the rest of them. They'd spent many a weekend camped out down here, fishing, knocking back beers and partying in their younger years. However, now it no longer held the same attraction as it had before. The river wasn't deep but fast moving. Although due to the plummeting temperatures, areas of the river had frozen over. As they made it to the banks of the river, he laid Sara down on the snow-covered ground and glanced up at a few spiny trees that no longer held leaves.

"Is there another way around?" Jesse asked.

"Not unless you want to head back to the road. We need to cross it."

"And how do you suppose we do that? She's shot, it's freezing fucking cold and we are miles from Keene."

"I told you what road to take," Damon replied.

"I'm not from here. They all look the same," Jesse shot back.

Before heading across, Damon decided to bury Sara. It wouldn't be easy as the ground was hard from the cold and he had no tools but he wasn't going to leave her above ground.

"Give me a hand," he said to Jesse as he went over to a large tree and snapped off a branch. He then searched for a spot near the water's edge where the earth was waterlogged and soft. It took about ten minutes to find an area where the soil was loose enough that he could scrape and scoop it out. Jesse assisted him and over the course of half an hour they scraped away until there was just enough space to roll Sara's body into. They covered her and he made a makeshift cross out of old sticks and vine.

When he was done, he stood back and dropped his head to say a short prayer. Damon wasn't religious, but he did believe there was something behind creation.

Once he was done, he went over to Maggie. She'd taken a seat on an outcropping of rock and was trying to get a better look at the wound.

"Let me see," he said.

He pulled back her bloodied jacket and examined the front, then the back of her shoulder. The bullet hadn't gone all the way through which wasn't good.

"Get it out of me," she said.

"No, we need to minimize the bleeding and get you to a doctor."

"And what about shock?" Jesse said.

"Right now the main threat is bleeding and infection."

"Yeah so take the bullet out."

"Listen, we could end up doing more damage. Toss over the backpack," he said to Jesse. He slipped it off and handed it to him. Damon dug around inside hoping that Elliot had given them something, anything they could use for this. There was all manner of shit inside, mostly basic items to start a fire, purification tablets, a hunting knife that had tools inside the handle, a plastic bag that contained some bandages, a tarp, a flint match lighter, a whistle, a local map, a canteen for water, a small can of lighter fluid, a first-aid kit, a flashlight, a small hand-crank radio and some MREs. That was it. It was no 72-hour bug-out bag but it would certainly come in handy to get them through the night. Damon pulled out the bandages, bunched them up and applied pressure to the wound.

"We need to elevate your arm. This isn't going to be comfortable, but it's going to prevent you from bleeding out until we can make it back to town. It's getting dark and there's no way we're going to be able to see what the hell we are doing even with a flashlight. Jesse, take off her top."

He hesitated for a second and glanced at Maggie.

"Come on. We're all adults here."

Damon took out more of the bulky dressing and placed it against the wound. He placed Maggie's hand over the top. "Just keep applying pressure to that. If that doesn't work we might have to create a tourniquet."

"How do you know to treat this?"

He continued to keep his hand on the bandages, then stopped for a second and with the other hand pulled up his sleeve to expose a wound to his upper right arm. "Back when I was sixteen, I was out hunting, miles from a hospital with my old man, I mean my foster parent. Anyway I was in the wrong place at the wrong time and got clipped. My old man was in the military. I was freaking out thinking I was going to die, but he was calm and didn't even bat an eye. I swear there was very little that rocked that man. Anyway, he patched me up. We made it back, they took it out, and the rest is history."

"Where are your parents?"

"Mother is dead, father is in Keene still."

"You didn't seem eager to get back to see him."

Damon nodded. "We never really saw eye to eye."

"When did you leave home?"

"Eighteen. As soon as I was old enough to leave the system."

He pressed down on the arm and Maggie winced.

"Where are your real parents?"

"No idea."

"You didn't want to know?"

"Anyone who leaves me behind isn't worth my time."

Jesse nodded and glanced out at the river. He looked around. They needed to cross the river, start a fire and get warm. A cold wind nipped at his skin and he shivered.

"We are going to freeze to death, aren't we?" Jesse asked.

"We'll be fine."

Jesse chuckled as he pulled his jacket tight. "Two weeks ago I would have never imagined I'd be stuck in some backwoods town of upstate New York on the run from a group of lunatics."

Damon checked the wound again. "There, that should

do it. We'll just keep changing out the bandage. Once we get back to town, we'll get a vehicle and make our way back to Lake Placid to get you treated."

She nodded as he got up and observed the rushing water. They'd not had a lot of snow that January but with the temperature below freezing, it wouldn't take them long to suffer from hypothermia. Damon knew Cole well enough to know that he wouldn't wait around for him to show; he'd come after him. That was just his way. Even before the world went to shit he didn't let things slide if they could be handled immediately. His biggest concern was once they crossed the river they'd have to start a fire to dry off their clothes and get warm. At night that fire was going to be visible. They might as well have shot a flare into the air as it was going to be that easy to find them. Damon looked up the river. It was stony, and he knew there were spots along the way that were easier to cross because it was shallow but in the dark it would be hard to see and they needed to go south.

"Ready to do this?"

Jesse nodded as he hauled Maggie to her feet. They began wading into the frigid waters. It was only deep enough to come up to their knees, but that wasn't what bothered him. The bottom wasn't flat, and he remembered his father slipping on the stones when they were fly-fishing in it. That was in the summer. In the winter it could mean a death sentence. He stumbled a little and braced himself against a rock, his hands reaching into the freezing cold water. Slivers of ice that hadn't properly formed drifted downstream. It was a slow process, but they eventually made it to the other side. Damon pulled off his boots and emptied the water, then squeezed out his waterlogged socks while the others did the same. The only upside to the river separating the road from the wilderness was that it meant if Cole followed, he'd have to get wet too, unless of course he entered from the south end. Damon had to hope he had more sense than to pursue them at night.

As the sun began to wane behind the trees and the last sliver of light vanished, the wilderness was blanketed by darkness. Damon switched the flashlight on and led the way, deeper into God's country.

Now they just had to survive the night.

Chapter 11

Richie Summers didn't make it. The poor guy had taken a bullet to the head and was killed instantly. The only consolation was that he didn't suffer and gave his life while trying to help an officer. That was more than some would get. As soon as Gary laid eyes on the suspects, he knew who they were — Mark Browning, Keith Wendell, Lee Warren and Debbie Mundal. They'd had several run-ins with the law over the past few years and had been charged with drug misdemeanors. After retrieving the Jeep, they carted away the sole survivor — Keith Wendell — to be medically treated.

Elliot would have gladly finished him off instead of wasting precious resources on his sorry ass but Gary intervened. Ten minutes later they were on the road heading for the Adirondack Medical Center.

"What is it?" Gary asked glancing at Elliot as he drove along the cluttered streets.

"He kidnapped a police officer, his buddy killed Richie and you want to waste supplies keeping him alive?"

"We're not animals."

"No, but they are."

"Elliot, if we lower our standards because others do, where does that leave us?"

He didn't even have to think to answer that one. "Alive."

He snorted and glanced over his shoulder. He was riding shotgun while Laura, Keith, Officer Jackson and Kong were in the back.

"You're not seeing the bigger picture here," Gary said glancing out the window. "We've got to work together to build this community back to where it was before. That means keeping law and order in place. We wouldn't have killed him in cold blood before and we're not going to do that now."

"I'm just saying."

"Well don't. You're not the one in charge."

"Neither are you," Elliot spat back.

"Unless things get worse, I'm still an officer bound to my duties."

"Oh cut the bullshit, Gary. Look around you, man. Things have already got worse. There are dead bodies in the streets, homes on fire, stores have been looted, people are killing and kidnapping, and we haven't even seen the half of what's going on behind doors as you're too busy trying to protect the little you have."

"Is that any different from what you're trying to do? You speak the big game, Elliot, but the fact is you are just as worried as these people. Now, sure the odds are against us and things are bad but if we work—"

"If you say work together one more time, you can get out and walk back to the department."

He chuckled. "Actually, this Jeep belongs to the police department."

Elliot shook his head. He was splitting hairs now.

When they arrived at the Emergency Center off Church Street, Gary had already radioed ahead to have an officer stationed there. The low-slung brick structure was surrounded by trees and rolling hills. Before the lights went out, they offered emergency services between 8 a.m. and 11 p.m. Beyond that residents had to go to Saranac Lake. Though now they were operating around the clock on a skeleton crew that consisted of two doctors and four nurses. To say they were overworked would have been an understatement. The number of attacks on people had increased and with it, the need for medical attention.

Jackson had suffered a mild concussion where they'd beaten him over the head. He had little idea of what had taken place only that he remembered driving up to the Olympic Center and getting out.

"Get him out," Elliot said to Gary as they waited in the Jeep.

Gary hopped out and went through the process of handing him over to a nurse. He updated the officer and three volunteers offering security and told them that he was to be kept updated on Keith's progress. Once he was fit to leave, he'd be placed in the local jail, which wasn't exactly a smart move as it was already filled to capacity. A volunteer helped the nurse place him in a wheelchair.

As they began to roll him away, Elliot brought his window down. "Hold up a minute."

Gary looked over wondering what he wanted.

"Who put you up to this?" Elliot asked.

The guy clutched his leg and refused to look at Elliot, so he got out of the truck.

"This is not the time, Elliot," Gary said stepping between them.

"You heard them yourself." He pushed past him and stopped the nurse from heading in. "What were you going to get for doing this?"

"Look, man, I don't know what the hell you are on about," Keith said.

Elliot reached down and gripped his leg, pushing a thumb into his wound causing him to scream in agony. "A good man died back there because of you!"

The nurse tried to stop him as did Gary who lunged forward and knocked Elliot back.

"You want to play games?" Elliot yelled as Gary hauled

him away. The nurse rolled Keith into the safety of the medical center while Gary kept a firm grip on Elliot's ballistic vest.

"What is your problem, man?"

"Someone put them up to this."

"Yeah, no doubt it was one of their dealers. We have bigger things to deal with right now."

"Like helping people like that asshole?"

"Just get in the Jeep, Elliot," Gary said as he made his way around to the passenger side. Elliot understood what Gary was trying to do. He wanted to remain professional and keep up appearances. He wanted to reassure the people of Lake Placid that even though the country had come under attack, order and safety was still their top priority but what he wasn't willing to admit was their control was slowly slipping.

* * *

Cole sat composed while Tyron ranted about never trusting Damon. "I told you about him, didn't I?" he said to Magnus then tossed Cole a dirty look. "I said you couldn't trust him and I was right."

"Sit down, Tyron, you're making my blood pressure go up."

Magnus and Tyron were feeding off each other and only making the situation worse. Sure it was bad, but he'd figured Damon wouldn't have gone along with the plan, so he'd planned on having Tyron go with him to Lake Placid. But now that was all screwed up!

The sound of a vehicle caught Tyron's attention, and he hurried over to the window.

"Sawyer's back."

"Well let's at least hope he brought Pete with him as I'm starving," Cole said.

"How can you think of food at a time like this?" Magnus said.

"Sit down and relax. It's all going to work out," Cole said gazing into the fire while smoking a cigarette. He was lying but he couldn't let them see weakness. That's how mutiny happened. As soon as a crew saw a weak link, they would be all over that like a cat on a fish. No, he had to maintain a strong front even if he was floundering. The truth was he thought it would be easier than this, but he was beginning to think that sticking a gun in someone's face might be the only option he had. It wasn't like he was against it, but in running his business he only once had to resort to violence to send a clear message. He looked at the others, they were like wild penned-in animals just waiting to be released. If they didn't have something to sink their teeth into soon, he'd lose their trust and right now that was all he had.

"I'm telling you, he knows who killed my cousins. That's why he bolted. In fact I wouldn't be surprised if it was him," Magnus said.

"It's possible," Tyron replied, only inciting Magnus even more.

Sawyer entered the tavern and the first thing he did was head over to the bar and pour a drink.

"Where's Pete?" Devin asked.

"I stopped them," he said knocking back his drink and pouring another. Cole got up and crossed the room.

"What?"

"I shot one of them. The girl, and took out a tire, and I must have hit the gas tank as it was leaking and they pulled off near Upper Jay. Two of them headed into the forest."

"That's my boy!" Magnus said slapping him on the back. "At least one of us is thinking straight," he said before looking at Cole.

"And Damon?"

"Had to turn back, he was firing at me. The Scout is pretty shot up but still working."

"And Sara?"

"I didn't see her get out."

Cole ran a hand over his face and walked back to the fireplace. He leaned against the stone wall and pulled out a cigarette. Just a little bit of nicotine, something to ease his nerves. It wasn't meant to be like this. He figured Damon would return, they'd hash out their differences over the drug bust and go on with business as though nothing had ever happened. They had a history. It was stronger than eight months in jail, wasn't it? He lit the cigarette between his lips and was questioning if he'd been too pushy when Magnus walked over and stood in front him.

"We're going after him, aren't we?" Magnus asked.

Cole jabbed the air with his cigarette. "Let's put a pin in that right now."

"Are you kidding?"

"I'm just saying, let's not be hasty."

"Hasty? You heard him. She's hurt and they don't have wheels. We've got them. I say we head out now before they try to work their way back to town."

"It's dark out, we'll go at first light."

"No, we'll go now."

Magnus was pushing for a response. Cole could have lashed out and made him understand through brute force, but he figured helping him see how illogical it was would suffice.

"And how do you expect to find them? It's dark, and even darker in Sentinel."

"It's also nineteen degrees outside. They're going to need to stay warm. Which means we just need to follow the smoke, find the fire and we've got them. He'll expect us to come in the morning. If we go now, we have the advantage."

"Jesus, Magnus. You don't even know if he's responsible for Trent's death. You're reaching and quite frankly, it's fucking annoying," Cole said walking away from him and heading into the kitchen to see what he could drum up for dinner. Magnus followed him; he wasn't going to let it go.

"You know, Cole, I do everything you say. All of us do. We've risked our necks countless times for you over the years. Hell, that could have been me that day Damon took the fall. Now all I'm asking for is one damn thing. I want answers and he damn well has them, and if he doesn't maybe the other two do. So if you want to stay here be my guest but I'm taking Sawyer and Devin and Tyron with me to hunt down this prick."

Cole entered a large walk-in freezer

"That prick was our friend."

"No he wasn't. He was yours. We just put up with him." He paused as Cole came out of the freezer and tossed a few steaks on the counter then headed over to the pantry. "He never wanted to be in the drug business, and I told you countless times that one day it would come back and bite us in the ass and sure enough it has."

"For you, not for me."

Magnus picked up an unopened bottle of wine off the kitchen counter and tossed it across the room. It smashed against the wall with wine dripping down to the floor. "I'm tired of this shit. I'm leaving now."

As he headed back into the restaurant Cole followed him out.

"I'll go with you."

Magnus turned. "Yeah?"

"On one condition. No one harms him."

"I can't promise that."

"We need him."

"No we don't. We are done pussyfooting around. I'm

taking what I want, when I want and how I want and if anyone attempts to stop me." He pulled his firearm. "I hope they've made peace with their maker." He turned and headed toward the door. "Sawyer, Devin, Tyron, let's go."

Magnus swung the door open and headed out into the snowy night.

The others looked at Cole and shrugged. He had a feeling this would eventually happen. If it wasn't Magnus, it would have been someone else. He stood there for a few seconds before balling his fist and following after them. He had no choice. He didn't want Damon dead any more than he wanted to face this new existence but shit happened and he had to roll with it.

* * *

Tongues of fire cut into the darkness. Stones close to the fire had their socks draped over them so they could dry. Damon had led them to a small clearing in the woods that was close to a pond and yet far enough away from the river and highway. Maggie's thighs ached from trudging through the forest but it wasn't as bad as the pain in her shoulder. It was excruciating. Like anyone else she'd seen people get shot in the movies and on TV but she could never imagine it hurt this bad. It felt like someone was jabbing a searing hot poker in her shoulder. Damon had her position her arm upright, and he'd even wrapped a bandage so it held her arm in place. She was laying back against a tree and all three of them were laying on a tarp to keep the snow away from their bodies. Damon checked the socks. He collected hers and took a few minutes to put them back on her feet. The warmth felt good. They weren't completely dry but at least they weren't soaking wet.

"Thanks," she muttered.

Damon gave a thin smile before returning to put on his own socks.

"Can't you remove the bullet and cauterize it like they used to do in the old days?" Jesse asked.

"I could if she wants to get an infection. No, the bandages should do for now. It hasn't hit an artery otherwise she'd be dead by now. It's not heavy, but she needs it looked at. There's no telling what damage has been done to the bone."

"How long will take to heal?" she asked.

"I'm no doctor but if it's a clean shot, and it missed bone, nerves and artery — a couple of weeks."

"And if it gets infected?" she asked.

"You'll know in a matter of days."

She nodded and groaned. She'd broken her finger when she was eight years of age and remembered how badly it hurt. The pinkie had swollen up to three times its usual size and felt like the darn thing was going to pop. But that was nothing compared to this. She tried to take her mind off the pain by thinking of anything else but it was near impossible.

"I'm sorry about Sara," Maggie said.

Damon dropped his chin. She could see the anguish in his face. She was going to ask him more questions but he must have wanted to be alone as he got up and said he was going to collect water. As he walked away, she turned to Jesse.

"You think they'll come?"

He glanced off toward the pond where Damon was standing collecting water. "If they are, they better be prepared to die."

Chapter 12

The reality that she was gone hadn't sunk in until Maggie offered her sympathy. Sure he'd seen her lifeless body, felt her last breath against his skin but a part of him expected to wake up and find that it was just a bad dream — that all of this was nothing more than a concoction of his mind under duress. Damon crouched at the edge of the pond and filled up the metal canister with the cool water, he planned on tossing in one of the purifying tablets, then boiling it. Elliot had said it was crucial to filter and go through some long process of using pebbles, burlap and seven inches of thick soil, in order to remove fallout particles and get usable water. But that seemed like an awful lot of work when the chances were they wouldn't survive the winter.

"Smoke?" Jesse said coming up behind him. He turned to find him extending a pack of Marlboros.

Damon's brow furrowed. "You don't smoke."

"No, but I thought if I ever felt the urge at least I'd have a pack on hand."

The corner of Damon's lip curled. He reached for one and pulled a Zippo lighter from his pocket and singed the end. Jesse pocketed the pack.

Damon jabbed a finger at him. "You know you're odd."

"Colorful, I prefer."

Damon snorted. They stood on the banks of the pond looking out into the darkest night. A canopy of stars stretched above them, a reminder that some places were out of reach of humanity's destructive tendencies.

"You miss the city?" he asked blowing smoke out his nostrils.

"Right about now. Yeah," Jesse replied. "Hell, I'd even put up with my old job and listening to my neighbor drone about utter horseshit for twenty-four hours if it meant the world would go back to normal." He sighed. "Like I know it wasn't all rainbows and sunshine before the lights went out but at least I knew where I stood. You know?" He stuck his hands in his pockets and hunched his shoulders as a cold wind nipped at their ears.

"It might sound odd but I think we're safer here," Damon said.

Jesse laughed. "I'm pretty sure no one is going to be chasing anyone down 5th Avenue."

"You don't know that."

"Yeah, I do. That road on a normal day was clogged with traffic. No one is getting down there unless they're on foot."

"So you think you would have survived if you'd stayed?"

"Probably not but who knows? For all we know the National Guard may have moved in and set up secure locations. I imagine eventually we'll see military in these parts," Jesse said.

"I wouldn't bank on it. They'll stick to the cities. There's more supplies and resources to protect and if the country has come under attack and this isn't just some screw-up by the military, then maybe the lights will come back on."

Jesse shook his head.

"What?" Damon asked.

"Even if they manage to get the power grid on, it's going to take years before society returns to normal. The devastation of a nuke will have rippled out, killing thousands and causing untold chaos in cities and towns. How would they reel it back in?"

"Martial law. They'll enforce their rule over the public. Seizing of arms will be first, curfews will be put in place and arrests will be made."

"Yeah and who's going to do that?"

"There are over 800 U.S. bases dotted around the planet in 80 countries."

"Really?"

"At least according to my old man." Damon sniffed. "I figure those troops will make their way home."

There was silence for a minute.

"I thought you didn't talk to him?" Jesse asked.

"I don't but that didn't stop him from sending me

emails. And the worst part was there wasn't even an unsubscribe link."

They both laughed.

"What's the deal with you and him?"

Damon looked back toward the camp to check on Maggie. She was using Jesse's coat to stay warm while he suffered in silence. The things people did for love.

"I'll give you one guess."

"Cole?"

"Bingo!" He paused. "Yeah, Cole's reputation preceded him. Back when I was a youngster he didn't like me hanging out with him. Said he was bad news. I should have listened."

"So how did that create a problem?"

"I didn't agree with him at the time. Told him to keep his nose out of it. But he wouldn't listen. You see, he knew about Cole dealing drugs. It's a small town, word travels and by the time State Police show up, there was nothing to be found. It was always his word against Cole's. It didn't help that my father drank like a fish and had earned his own reputation. No one believed him. Anyway, he showed up one night when I was on a two-day coke binge. Well, words were exchanged, I ended up throwing a punch, and it didn't end well. Let's just leave at that."

"Everything is 20-20 in hindsight."

"That it is," Damon said.

There was quiet between them for a while, only the sound of wood crackling. Jesse looked over his shoulder. "You think she's going to be okay?"

"I've seen worse."

"Ah, that's comforting," Jesse said sarcastically.

"Tomorrow we'll head back to Keene. I know someone that can help."

"A doctor?"

"No, a vet."

"A vet?"

"Same kind of thing."

"Yeah if you're eighty pounds, have four legs and a snout. C'mon, are you kidding me?"

"I'm joking, Jesse. We'll drop in on my old man."

He cocked his head. "He's still in Keene?"

"I hope so."

Jesse's brow knit together. "When did you last see him?"

"Six years before I went inside."

"And you think he's going to help you?"

"No but we don't exactly have many options here, and he knows how to treat gunshot wounds."

"She needs medical attention, Damon, not someone with just enough knowledge." He looked over his shoulder toward Maggie. She was still gripping her shoulder and staring into the fire. The fire created shadows that danced against her features. Even in the dim light, she was attractive. He shivered in the cold.

"You're going to freeze to death," Damon said.

"I'll be fine."

He chuckled. "You like her?"

"Who?" Jesse asked.

"Jesse, I don't have a college degree but I'm not blind."

He jerked a thumb behind him.

"Who, Maggie? No."

"Jesse."

"Alright I admit she's pretty hot."

"You told her?"

"No. Not exactly the right time, is it?"

"When is?" Damon looked at him. "If there's anything this event has taught me, it's not to wait or hold off telling those that mean something to you, that you love them."

"Oh dude, that sounds like a bunch of gush to me," Jesse replied.

"Well, that's for you to decide." Damon flicked the remainder of his cigarette into the water. Jesse shivered again, his teeth chattering ever so slightly. A few more minutes passed before Damon screwed the cap on the canister.

"Look, I just wanted to say that I know what it feels like to lose someone."

Damon didn't reply. He was still processing it. Trying

to come to terms with it.

"Do you ever get over it?" Damon asked.

"No, you just learn to live with it."

He was just about to say one more thing when Maggie let out a high-pitched scream. "Jesse!"

They turned to find Jesse's coat on the ground and Maggie gone. Jesse was about to run back when Damon grabbed him and clamped his hand over his mouth. He pulled him to the ground and scanned the clearing with his rifle raking over the terrain. In a whisper he said, "They can't see us here. You run into that clearing and you are dead."

The edge of the pond was just over a small rise. From the campsite a person would have been hard-pressed to notice them as it was pitch-dark in the forest but from where they were positioned they could see the fire illuminating the clearing. They remained quiet. *Where are you?* They could hear movement. The crunching of twigs and underbrush. Someone hurrying and hushed voices.

That's when they heard him. "Damon! I know you can

hear me."

Cole. He'd figured he'd wait until morning. If he was honest, he should have anticipated this but they would have frozen to death if they hadn't started that fire.

"Listen to me. You've brought this on yourself. All I wanted was for you to work with me. This still doesn't need to end badly."

He wanted to scream back at him but they remained quiet. Replying would have only given away their position, and that was the only thing they had working for them. He didn't dare move just in case they were heard and spotted. There was no use trying to take them out. They had the darkness working against them and they were outnumbered five to two. He'd hunted animals growing up, but this was different. Sitting in a tree stand was one thing, pursuing armed individuals another. Jesse struggled within his grasp.

"You say anything, and we're dead," Damon whispered in his ear.

He listened as Cole continued.

"Now I won't harm this woman but I can't speak for the others. They want you dead. You hear me?" There was silence, except for the gentle lapping of water against the shore. "So this is your last chance. One more opportunity. That's all you get. Take it or leave it. What's it gonna be?"

"Shit. Shit!" he muttered under his breath. He was drawing him out. Giving him an ultimatum that he had to respond to even if he didn't agree.

"Jesse, you got your handgun?"

"Yeah."

"You remain here on the south side, I'm gonna shift position to the east and respond. They're gonna come for me. Okay? If they cross through that clearing — shoot. You got it?"

He nodded. Jesse patted him on the back and remained in a crouched position. He shuffled sideways like a crab along the shore making his way around. He kind of knew Cole wasn't going to give him a free ride, in which case he was going to make damn sure they didn't leave these woods without going down with him. His mind flashed to Sara. The look of shock in her eyes. The fear of knowing she was about to die. He used that image as fuel to drive him.

Damon moved around a tree and crouched down near a mossy boulder. His eyes had adjusted to the darkness and there he could make out the silhouette of Jesse's head bobbing up to take a look. He shifted position. As he made his way to another rock, he spotted Devin between the trees. He was pressed up against a pine and peeking out looking toward the fire with his rifle in preparation. *Where are you, Maggie?*

How they had managed to get the drop on them without hearing their approach was strangely impressive. Though he knew Magnus was an avid hunter and Cole had spent his fair share of time in the wilderness. There wasn't much else to do in their neck of the woods.

"Damon, I need an answer. What's it gonna be?"

He liked Devin, and he'd never done him wrong but as long as he was aligned with Cole, and holding a gun, he was as guilty as the rest of them. Without saying a word he pocketed his Glock and swung the rifle around and brought the scope to his eye. He pressed the fleshy part of his finger against the trigger and put Devin's head in the cross hair. His finger twitched and without missing a beat he squeezed. The round hit its mark and dropped him. They must have been close as he heard Cole yell.

"Damon! You've killed him."

"And you killed her!" he replied as he shifted ass and darted in and out of the trees, firing off a few more rounds in the hope that in their anger they would give chase and run out into the clearing giving Jesse a clear view. But they didn't. They were smarter than that. Now he knew he might have just signed Maggie's death warrant but the way he saw it, they were planning on killing them, anyway. Coming all the way up here in the middle of the night to offer him a second chance? No. That was never in the cards. At least now he'd leveled the playing field and reduced their numbers to four.

He took off running seeking cover in the massive pine

trees and evergreen foliage. He could hear them behind him calling out to one another. "He went that way."

"No, fan out."

"Where's the other one?" Tyron shouted.

"I don't see him."

Damon knew the area well. He and his father had spent many a weekend out there hunting deer. Hours of trekking through forest and waiting in tree stands gave him an appreciation for the vastness of the land. He'd learned to plot out the area using landmarks like outcroppings of rock or fallen trees, and of course the position of the sun and the moon.

He stayed low, running uphill toward a large gathering of boulders. It would give him a good view of the terrain below and provide ample cover. His throat was burning from moving so fast, and his adrenaline had blocked out the cold. He ducked behind a boulder and brought his rifle up looking downwind. He could have used night vision goggles, but he'd have to rely on the moon's light and his senses. Damon could hear voices and boots pounding the ground. He cleared away some snow from the top of a boulder and positioned his rifle waiting for someone to step into view. How had it come to this? Friends hunting friends? Or were they ever that to begin with?

There, he spotted Sawyer dashing from one tree to the next. He took aim and was about to squeeze off the trigger when a round tore up the ground behind. *Shit.* They'd spotted him. He slunk down and moved fast heading farther along the slope.

"Give up, Damon!" Cole yelled. "You're outnumbered."

He twisted around and caught sight of Magnus running at a crouch. He squeezed off two rounds, but neither hit their mark. It was tough to hit a running target, even harder in the dark. Cole and Tyron emerged from dense trees and burst across a clearing. Every couple of seconds he would see the muzzle flash of a gun as they opened fire in his direction. Rounds kicked up dirt off to his right, which led him to believe they were having as much of a hard time seeing him as he was with them. He rolled out of view and shifted ass again. The key was to keep moving. Never stay in one place, his father would tell him.

Chapter 13

The second town hall meeting for public input on the challenges facing Lake Placid residents was a bust. There were only forty-two people in attendance, and in a town of more than two thousand that was an awful turnout. It was a far cry from the first, two weeks ago, which saw the building bursting at the seams with everyone and their uncle wanting to voice their concerns and opinions. Now with no power, and an excessive amount of looting, it seemed that most of the town had concluded they were on their own. Mayor Hammond looked thinner, and even more stressed than before. He stood at the podium doing his best to address the increase in robberies, fires and violence and in some cases rape.

Rayna cast her eyes over worried faces and spotted Jill on the far side. She waved to her but Jill looked away. Twelve days spent inside the bunker with her and Gary had been brutal. She'd attempted speaking to Jill if only to create small talk but it had failed. While she hadn't said anything to Elliot, she knew that it was only a matter of time. Everyone in town was losing patience with each other and looking for any reason to argue.

Elliot had said he would be there but neither he nor Gary had shown. There had been moments that she'd thought of telling him but that would have only put them at odds with each other and right now what they were facing was more important. There was a time for everything and now wasn't it.

A tall man with a thick beard jabbed his finger in the air. "My daughter was raped, the guy who did it is still out there. I want to know, what is being done?"

"Yeah!" those in the crowd joined in.

Assistant Chief Ted Murphy stepped up to the mic and Hammond took a seat looking relieved that someone else wanted to be the sounding board.

"Sir, I understand your frustration and I want to reassure you that we are doing everything we can to protect and—"

The man laughed. "Protect? Where were your guys when she was dragged into an alley on the west side of town and brutalized?"

Someone else in the room stood up and told him to calm down. "The cops are doing the best they can. They are understaffed."

"Well their best is not good enough. I did not spend my entire life working and paying taxes to have to deal with this crap. Now I want real answers!"

Ted continued. "Sir, the only answer I can give you right now is that we are in the process of creating new officers to assist us. But it's not an easy or fast task. We are facing circumstances that have strained and buckled the infrastructure. We've lost three of our officers, one to a gunshot wound and the other two have abandoned their post."

"Oh that is great. And in the meantime what are we meant to do? You see because—"

"Maybe you should shut the hell up and let Ted speak!" a middle-aged man with a bald head rose to his feet and bellowed.

"I should what?" The man jabbed his finger. "Are you going to make me? Huh? Come on!" He charged over to confront the man and all hell broke loose. Fists flew and six other people tried to intervene but one of them got thumped in the face. The few officers there to provide security rushed in but only ended up getting mauled. It took another four people, including Rayna to restore order.

"Look, we understand your frustration but you need to be realistic about the situation that is before us. So I'm going to lay it out for you all. There is a good chance the power is not coming back up, which means we either work together or you leave the town. It's a simple as that. We have minimal vehicles, less than twenty people, some of whom I might add are volunteers involved in protecting and maintaining the peace. In fact most of them are out there right now in freezing cold weather because they want to help. None of them are paid. None of them are being treated any better than you. However, the difference between them and you is that those volunteers understand that the only way to survive this is to work together. So what's it going to be?" Ted asked.

Some guy got up and flipped him the bird and kicked a chair on the way out. Another grumbled under his breath, folded his arms and shook his head. As strange as it might have seemed, there would always be those who thought that the government and life owed them something while others didn't. No matter what the situation was some couldn't wrap their head around the fact that the infrastructure had been hamstrung by the power outage and that meant a drastic and immediate reduction in services provided. Jobs that were once given only to those that proved themselves were now being offered freely — the problem was few wanted to take them. It was dangerous; there was no pay or even fringe benefits. It was interesting to see who would roll up their sleeves and willingly help and who would stand back and expect to be waited on.

Rayna didn't know Ted that well. Like the previous

chief he kept to himself and the only times she'd seen him was at community events.

"If you have any questions, please see me after. If you're interested in helping, we are creating a list. All we ask is that you tell us if you've had any military or hunting experience. Preference will be given to those who know how to use a firearm, however we could really use anyone who has proven communication skills. I can't guarantee you anything and it will mean long hours but there will be the satisfaction of knowing you are helping this community. We currently need those who are willing to hunt for food."

"I'll hunt but I will want a larger portion," James Bolton said.

"We can discuss that."

"There's no discussion involved. If you want me onboard, you've got me but those are my terms."

"People, this is not about setting up terms. We aren't trading here."

"Of course we are. If you can't pay me money, then I

will want payment another way. I set the terms."

Ted narrowed his eyes. "See me after please."

Over the next few minutes questions were answered and some fears about raiders were relieved as Ted presented new ideas.

"Currently we have a lot of the elderly at the Olympic Center. If you don't wish to stay at home and you have a gas or solar generator, it's probably best you head for the center but be sure to bring the generator with you. There is already a strain on our current resources and with no food or fuel being delivered our supplies are dwindling by the day."

After half an hour they concluded the meeting and many of those in attendance signed up to help out while the rest began streaming out complaining. In the crowd Rayna singled out Jill and crossed the room to speak with her before she left.

"Jill!"

She looked at her out the corner of her eye and acted as if she hadn't heard. Rayna cut her off before she left.

"We need to talk."

"There is nothing to talk about."

"Of course there is. You hardly said a word to me inside the bunker."

She pursed her lips and looked past Rayna, not even wanting to look her in the eye.

"Please. We've been friends for a long time. All I want is five minutes of your time to explain as I'm guessing Gary didn't."

Her eyes lifted and then she nodded. "Outside."

They moved away from the crowd and exited the building. Outside it was freezing cold. The temperature had dropped again. They huddled in an area out of the wind. Rayna pulled her hood up and stuck her hands in her pockets.

"Nothing happened between me and Gary. Now I know you don't want to hear it, but he came on to me, not the other way around."

"He wouldn't do that," Jill said, shaking her head.

"Then you don't know him enough."

She was quick to react to that. "I've been married to him for over twelve years. I think I know my own husband."

"We all have our secrets."

"Not Gary. He's an open book."

"In his job, maybe, but he's not been honest with you. Did you even talk to him?"

"When did I have the time?"

Rayna frowned. "In the shelter?"

"Yeah, like we were going to have that discussion there."

"I'll be completely frank with you, Jill. After Elliot left, Gary would visit to check in and see that I was okay. His visits started to become more frequent. In no way did I lead him on."

"So you didn't have sex? Is that what you're saying?"

"No. God no. I would never do that to you or Elliot."

"Did you kiss him?"

Rayna breathed in deeply. "He kissed me, and I pushed away and told him I was not interested."

She scrutinized her. "You didn't allow it even once?"

There it was, the question that she had hoped she wouldn't ask.

"There was one time but—"

Without missing a beat Jill slapped her across the face. Rayna touched her cheek, which was stinging. It felt even worse with the freezing wind nipping at it. "I guess I deserve that except you didn't allow me to finish." She paused for a second to see if Jill was going to react again. "The second time he tried to kiss me I had a lot to drink, I was alone. But I swear as your friend, Jill, I pushed him away after and told him I didn't want him coming around anymore. That I couldn't do it because of you and more specifically because of Elliot."

Jill narrowed her eyes. "Have you told Elliot?"

"No."

She scoffed. "And yet you have the nerve to tell me that I should chat with my husband?"

"You should if you value your marriage."

She stabbed her finger in Rayna's face. "Don't you

dare talk to me about marriage values!"

"Jill, I know you're pissed, but I didn't want it and every time he has tried to show affection I have pushed him away."

"Has? You mean he's continued?"

"Attempted I think is a better word."

Jill crossed her arms and shook her head in disbelief. "I've done everything for him. It's because I can't give him kids, that's why."

"It's not, Jill."

"Oh so he told you?"

She sighed and looked toward the entrance. Several people had stepped out and were lighting cigarettes. They glanced over and she turned her back.

"In a roundabout way."

"And what way would that be?"

"That's not for me to say."

"If you're truly my friend, you will tell me."

She dipped her chin. There was no easy way to say it without making her feel bad.

"Tell me!" she said raising her voice and getting the attention of the few outside.

"I can't. You need to hear it from him." She'd already stirred up the pot. If she told Jill what Gary had said, it would have devastated her. Although he loved his wife, he'd come to view her as not much more than a friend. He was no longer attracted to her. There was no way Rayna was going to tell her that.

Jill looked away. "Don't ever come over to our house again, and if you see me on the street, don't speak to me."

"Jill."

She turned and hurried away, and Rayna was sure she heard her cry.

"Mom?" Lily said from behind her. Rayna turned to find her standing nearby.

"How long have you been there?"

"A minute or two."

"What did you hear?"

"What?"

Rayna reached down and in a chaotic state of mind

took hold of her daughter by the arms. "What did you hear?"

Lily cowered. "I didn't hear anything. You're scaring me, Mom."

Rayna released her and backed up a little. In all honesty she was afraid of her kids finding out. Afraid that Elliot would discover it and then treat her the way Jill had. She'd just got him back. She shook her head despondently. "Go get your brother and let's go."

"He's not with you?"

"Stop playing, Lily. Get Evan and let's leave."

"I thought he was with you. That's why I came out."

Confused, Rayna hurried back into the town hall and began calling his name. "Evan?" There were only four people inside one of whom was Ted Murphy. He noticed her concern and walked over.

"Rayna, everything okay?"

"My son, I can't seem to find him."

"Well, I'm sure he hasn't gone far. It's too damn cold out. What's his name?"

"Evan."

"Okay, I'll check the bathroom and have a couple of the officers look outside."

"Evan!"

Panic sank in as her worst fear took hold. She'd done everything she could to protect the kids and now this? She dashed into the different offices calling his name while Lily did the same. Already feeling overwhelmed by her talk with Jill she couldn't hold back the tears from streaking her face. "Evan!"

Their voices echoed as five people tried to locate him.

When he emerged from a back room with a look of surprise on his face, she felt a wave of relief hit her, while at the same time anger welled up. "Where have you been?"

"I was just…"

She didn't care. All that mattered was he was back.

The sudden realization of the situation bore down on her; another reminder that they were living in dangerous times and that meant nowhere was safe.

Chapter 14

Jesse was certain he would die in those godforsaken woods. The steady staccato of gunfire continued for what felt like an hour but was probably closer to thirty minutes. After witnessing the death of one of the attackers he'd waited until they began pursuing Damon before he broke away from the water's edge and changed position. When he reached the dead guy on the ground, he tucked his Glock into his waistband and scooped up the man's AR-15 along with extra ammo. He yanked the magazine and checked it, then made sure there was a round in the chamber before joining the fight.

They may have been outnumbered but if he could offer additional support, maybe Damon would have a better chance of taking them out. He knew his shooting accuracy was shit, and despite the few lessons he'd learned from Elliot while in the bunker he still felt wet behind the ears. Jesse sprinted from one tree to the next and opened fire. Once his pals knew they were taking fire from the south and the west the gunfire stopped. He saw movement between the trees then heard the sound of boots growing distant. It was hard to tell if it was them or Damon. He squinted into the darkness shivering. His fingers were almost numb from the cold.

"Damon?" he yelled then moved position again hoping to God that he wasn't dead. He pressed his body against a tree and fired off another round. He was just about to dart to another when a hand clamped over his mouth pulling him to the ground. As he turned to face his attacker, Damon's face came into view. He put a finger up to his lips to get him to be quiet. They remained there for several minutes until there was nothing but the sounds of the forest.

Without saying a word Damon pointed to a cluster of boulders. Staying low they made their way over and remained there for another five minutes before Damon went to check if they were gone. He returned a minute later.

"I think we're in the clear. It's okay."

"It's not okay. They have Maggie," Jesse said rising to his feet determined to pursue them. Damon grasped him by his jacket.

"And they won't hurt her."

"You don't know that," he said shrugging him off.

"Yes I do. They had no intention of killing us tonight."

"Uh, yes they did."

"If they did, you would be dead by now. They want her. They want leverage. That's why they took Sara to begin with."

"Who cares?"

Damon grabbed him again.

"If you go after them now you'll just wind up dead."

Jesse paced back and forth, trying to get a grip on the situation.

"We'll grab our stuff and head back to Keene, find my old man. He'll be able to help."

"Help? We don't have time for a family reunion,

Damon."

"Jesse, we need to get a vehicle, and head back to Lake Placid and get Elliot and Gary involved."

"There's no time for that."

"It's a forty-minute drive, there and back."

"Yeah, and in that time she could die."

"You're not listening. They won't kill her. They need her as leverage. They're down one man and that little chat I had with them back at the tavern was all about recruiting others. That's why they've retreated. They can't afford to lose any more." He trudged off and Jesse followed. They made their way back to Devin's lifeless body. Damon crouched and went through his pockets. They were empty.

"Did you know him well?" Jesse asked.

"Yeah. We went to school with each other. Damn shame." He shook his head and returned to the campsite. Jesse scooped up his coat and held it for a second thinking about Maggie. She was probably scared out of her mind. He glanced at Damon. He might have thought he knew what his pals were like, but that was before law and order went out the window.

"How long did they know Sara?" Jesse asked.

"Since she was a kid."

"And yet they shot her?"

"Magnus shot her. He's a different breed."

"Well that's comforting to know. I'm sure Maggie is in good hands then," he said before kicking an empty MRE bag into the fire. He couldn't hide his frustration and he was tired of confronting people who had nothing better to do than kill others. He was beginning to think that he should have stayed in New York, at least there he didn't have to think about anyone else but himself. In the short time he'd known Maggie he'd come to view her as more than just a friend.

"Cole won't let him harm her."

"Oh no of course he won't because he did a stellar job of protecting Sara."

"That was different."

"Was it? Or are you just too blind to the fact that your

pals are lunatics?"

"Just grab your shit and let's get out of here. We have a lot of ground to cover."

Jesse scooped up the bag and stuffed it with the tarp, water canteen and knife. After putting his coat back on he slipped his arms through the straps and put it behind his back. Damon yawned, went down to the edge of the pond and splashed some water over his eyes.

"You might wanna do the same."

"I'm fine."

"I'm exhausted," Damon replied.

"Then we sleep. If you're right, we don't have anything to worry about." Jesse said, trying to gauge Damon's reaction. Did he even give a shit about Maggie?

Damon continued. "We'll freeze to death out here."

Jesse stopped following him and stared at him. "What? You said we were camping out here for the night, now you change your mind?"

"I didn't know it was going to get this cold, alright?"

The temperature had dropped and there was an awful

wind blowing through the trees. It cut through his coat chilling him to the bone. New York winters were brutal at the best of times but this was insane. Damon started to jog. "Come on, it will keep you warm. We'll get there sooner."

"How far is it?"

"By foot? Less than two hours."

"Are you serious?"

"About jogging or the time it's gonna take?"

"Both."

He nodded and pressed on. Jesse picked up the pace thinking about what was going on with Maggie.

* * *

Back at the tavern, Magnus was enraged. "We had them right there."

"Yeah and you would have probably died there. I told you before we went out that it was a stupid idea. It's too dark and if these temperatures drop any further, we'd freeze to death."

Sawyer was busy tossing logs of wood into the fireplace

while Tyron stood by the window gazing out.

"I swear you ever pull that shit again I'll…" Magnus began to say.

"You'll what?" Cole said bringing out his gun tapping it against his leg. He'd had enough of his shit. In fact he was at his breaking point and more than ready to kill him if he had to send a message to the other two. He was beginning to think that was the only way through this now. Not trading. Not negotiating. Just doing whatever was necessary.

He hopped over the bar and pulled out a twenty-year-old bottle of malt and cracked it open. He just needed something to take off the edge. He didn't bother pouring himself a glass, he knocked it back straight from the bottle then set it on the counter and glared at Magnus. Back in the Sentinel Wilderness, Magnus would have stayed if he hadn't threatened to leave him there. That was his problem, he didn't know when to choose his battles. He was like a wild dog that knew only one thing and that would eventually get him killed. It was part of the reason he'd hired him in the first place. Unlike the others he hadn't known Magnus since he was a kid. He'd been introduced to him through Sawyer. Their relationship had always been tumultuous. Maybe it was because the others knew where Cole was coming from, or perhaps he didn't like to follow. His drug business had taught him that some people in the world were leaders, and the rest were followers. There really wasn't any in-between. Sure, some might say they weren't followers but their actions always revealed the truth.

"I can't believe we left Devin out there," Tyron said glancing at him.

"Get used to it. Burying the dead is a waste of energy."

"You want to tell us what the plan is?" Sawyer said as he stoked the fire.

"Plan?"

"Well I hope Devin didn't die for nothing."

"The plan hasn't changed."

Magnus scoffed dropping down on the sofa and pulled out a pack of smokes. He banged it against his hand and placed one between his lips. "Yeah, come on, Cole, tell us your grand plan. We're all just sitting on the edge of our seats. It's gotta be good if you were in such a hurry to race back. Or perhaps that was fear I smelled in the forest."

Magnus was pushing his buttons. If it weren't for the fact that they were down one man, he would have put a bullet in his head. He was sick of his shit.

"It hasn't changed. We're just going to tweak it a little." Cole looked at the girl. She was sitting against the wall staring at them while gripping her shoulder. He walked over to her and crouched down. "How about you tell us what kind of setup you have back in Lake Placid, and if you know anything about the death of my friend's cousins? It might work in your benefit to tell us now."

She spat in his face, and Magnus laughed.

"She's a feisty one. A woman like that only understands one thing and I think you're lacking in that department," he said before laughing again. Cole glared at him then turned back to the girl. He wiped the spit from his face with the back of his sleeve and looked at her.

"Looks like that dressing of yours needs replacing."

"It's fine," she said through gritted teeth.

"Then you won't mind me taking a look."

She shook her head. He grabbed her wrist and dug his fingernails into her skin until she cried out and released her grip on the bandage.

"Um. That does not look good. But you know what, I think I have just the thing for it. Stay right here."

He got up and the other three eyed him as he walked into the kitchen and started digging around in the cupboard for a tool he'd seen earlier that day.

"There it is!"

When he returned, he was holding a kitchen blowtorch that was used to create that crunchy sugar on the top of crème brûlée. He released the safety switch on the back and as soon as she saw it she cowered back. "No. No!"

"It's okay, it's going to hurt like a bitch but it's better than bleeding out." He stooped down and pushed his hand against her chest to keep her against the wall. She flailed around trying to prevent him from getting near her. "Sawyer, Tyron. Hold her down."

As they came over she went berserk and fought back but it was pointless. Within seconds they had her on the floor and Cole was sitting on her stomach. He hit the ignition switch on the back and a large blue flame burst forth.

"Hold her still."

She thrashed around screaming at the top of her voice and that was without even getting the flame near her. Cole removed the bandages and brought the flame down and began cauterizing the wound. Her screams echoed and then within seconds she blacked out from the pain. He pulled back and placed it on the counter and then gave Sawyer a hand lifting her onto the sofa.

"You know that wasn't helpful," Magnus said sitting there with his feet up and gazing at his half-smoked cigarette. He rolled it between his fingers then glanced at Cole.

"And you would know because?"

"It's basic 101 medical care."

Cole snorted. "Says the expert."

"No, my mother was a nurse for ten years."

"Worked in the past," Sawyer said.

"Yeah until they figured out it can lead to infection."

"Like you care," Cole said.

"I don't, I'm just saying."

"Well don't. Keep your trap shut."

Cole looked at the girl one more time before heading into the back to snort a line of coke. He was losing his grip on the group and they were beginning to see that. If he didn't take action and demonstrate that he was still in control, they would soon lose confidence, if they hadn't already.

* * *

Both of them were shivering like crazy when they made it onto Irish Hill Road. Damon's thighs were burning from jogging. They'd stopped a couple of times on the way but only for five minutes to catch their breath and then continued on. Time was ticking and it would soon be morning. Once daylight arrived, Cole would reevaluate the situation. Although he wouldn't tell Jesse, he knew the chances of Maggie staying alive were slim.

His foster father was living in a used twenty-seven-foot Airstream trailer that was parked on a large lot of land belonging to a friend of his. After losing his wife to cancer he'd sold their three-bedroom home and most of his belongings and downsized and purchased the trailer. He'd wanted to get off the grid and live a minimalist lifestyle and he'd done that to some degree.

"Is he even here?"

"Only one way to find out."

When they arrived at the two-story home belonging to his father's friend, Amos Jones, they circled around back and saw a yellow light on inside the trailer's windows, and a solar generator churning away. The trailer itself sat back in the yard on top of bricks as one of the tires was flat. There was a dense forest that pressed up against it. He stopped about forty yards away and took a deep breath to prepare himself for his father's bullshit.

"You okay?" Jesse asked.

Damon swallowed hard and took a second to gather his thoughts. His mind was flooded with the final argument. Would he still remember that? It wasn't all bad times. He'd taken him hunting when he was a kid, taught him a lot about life and standing on his own two feet. Even though they hadn't seen eye to eye. It had been so many years since they'd met face to face. He fully expected him to not open the door. Reluctantly he approached and rapped his knuckles against the steel. He saw a shadow inside move to the window; a blind was pulled down then he heard him approach. The door swung wide and Damon stepped back.

"Hey Dad."

Chapter 15

Foster Goodman learned about the screw-up over the radio. Since seven that morning, he'd been a bag of nerves. He crushed the cigarette under his boot before heading into the medical center. No one from the department had shown up at his door which led him to believe the sole survivor hadn't said anything yet.

It had to stay that way.

After killing Chief Wayland he'd been horrified by what he'd done and paranoid of being caught but as the days passed, he began to relax. The fact was the cops didn't have the means or the resources to throw at a murder investigation.

It got him thinking about all the ways that he could use the country's situation to his advantage. At first it was small things like taking items from homes that were meant to be brought back to the Olympic Center for storage and distribution. From there he stepped up to stealing pills in order to pay drug addicts to do a few tasks. But that wasn't enough. As long as someone was in charge of who got what and who did what, he'd remain at the bottom of the totem pole. The only way to change that was to cut the head off the snake and he assumed once Chief Wayland was gone the others would fall in line. That was his mistake. Seeing Ted Murphy standing there spouting bullshit to the residents with a smug expression made him sick. He was just like Wayland, a man on a power trip. He knew that the moment he'd stepped up to the podium and introduced himself as the current chief of police things wouldn't change. Killing one wasn't enough.

Foster passed the officer inside the entranceway of the medical center. He noted several nurses darting from one patient to the next. It was a chaotic scene and foolish at the same time. The nurses were so preoccupied and overwhelmed by the need they didn't even acknowledge him. He felt like a ghost walking those hallways searching for Keith Wendell. In many ways he was, nothing more than a shell of a man. When Foster located Keith he was propped up in a bed with his eyes closed. He entered the room, shut the door behind him, and then closed the blinds.

The noise woke him.

"Foster?"

"How are you, Keith?"

"It was those damn cops. I don't know how they found us."

"Um, I have an idea."

Using drug addicts to set the wheels in motion on what he had planned for the town wasn't his first choice, but their desperation was just too hard to pass up. Foster pulled out of his pocket a container of OxyContin. "Thought you could use these? You know, for all the trouble you went through."

Keith's eyes widened, he swallowed and then got this wide grin on his face. Foster unscrewed the cap and shook out a couple into his hand but as he went to give the pills to him he closed his hand. Keith looked perplexed.

"First, I need to know something. Did you say anything to the cops?"

"No, Foster. They asked, but I didn't say anything."

"You sure?"

"Yeah, I swear on my mother's life."

What a lowlife, Foster thought.

"And the others?"

"Dead. They never had a chance, those bastards shot them. I was lucky to survive."

"And Jackson?"

"He didn't know what hit him. Actually they brought him in here."

"Where?"

He shrugged and kept eyeing his hand like a dog wanting its treat. "I don't know. You think I can have those?"

Foster looked at the tube going into his arm. "They got you on morphine?"

"Yeah. But not enough." He made a gesture to the pills.

"So you're in a lot of pain?"

"Yeah, yeah, can I get those?"

"Well then maybe you need more than two. You want more?"

"Yeah just leave the bottle."

"Sure, I'll leave it on the side table. Hey, let me get you a drink of water."

He turned toward a cabinet on the far side of the room that had several unopened bottles of water. Foster scooped one up. He unscrewed the top then placed it by his bedside table. Next he took out the bottle of pills, shaking out everything that was inside.

"Open up."

Keith frowned. "I just need two."

"That's fine. Open up."

Confused but driven by his need for the drugs he opened his mouth. Foster clamped his full hand over the top of his mouth, then squeezed his cheeks and with the other hand grabbed the water and poured it down his throat. He struggled to get Foster's hand off him but

Foster just kept slapping his hands away. His heart rate monitor started speeding up. He knew he only had minutes before a nurse would be in, so he pulled out the pillow from under his head and brought it down over his face and held it there as Keith flailed like a fish. His hands clawed at Foster's chest. Foster kept moving to avoid him. When the unit started beeping, he pulled the plug on it with his other hand and kept the pillow on his face until he stopped moving. Then, calmly he placed the pillow back under his head and crossed to the door. He glanced out but there was no security, no nurses rushing to his aid. Why? They were overwhelmed. Swamped. There were far more patients than emergency staff.

Foster strolled out and began heading down the hallway. When he reached the end he was about to turn when he spotted Officer Westin and Elliot Wilson heading his way. He shot back from the corner and entered the first room on his right. He closed the door just slightly and waited for them to turn and go back. Behind him an older woman in her late eighties was lying in bed with a mask over her face.

He squinted and a flash of memories came back to him of his own mother.

Right then and there a wave of guilt washed over him. He pushed it from his mind as he watched them go by. He waited a few more seconds and then darted out and hurried away.

* * *

Elliot had finally convinced Gary to go with him to speak with Keith. All night he'd been tossing and turning, thinking about what he'd heard on the way into the home. Someone had put them up to it and he was determined to find out.

"And so he told me last night he wants to see me this morning, something about a list that he's put together. You know, men and women in town that he wants to be officers." He sighed. "And get this, he says the first order of business will be to remove anyone in the town that isn't a local."

"He just wants to throw them to the curb?"

"That's about it."

"And what did you say?" Elliot asked, as they got closer to room 212.

"I told him he was out of his mind. It's not like they've got anywhere to go." He shook his head. "I tell you, Elliot, having Wayland die was the worst thing that could happen."

"You don't think Ted's behind his death, do you?"

Gary made a pfft sound. "I know it sounds bad but I wouldn't put it past him. Even when Wayland was alive Murphy thought he was the chief."

Gary pushed through the door and entered Keith's room.

"What the hell?" He hurried over and placed his fingers on the side of his neck. Elliot saw all the pills spilling out his mouth along with vomit. Gary turned his head on the side and scraped out the pills with his fingers, then started shouting for a nurse. Elliot assisted by doing chest compressions.

Even though Gary was bellowing loudly, no nurses

arrived. He left the room while Elliot continued to give compressions. Slowly he stopped and stepped back as Gary returned. "What are you doing?"

"He's gone, Gary."

Gary didn't believe him. He hurried over and continued as a doctor and a nurse came into the room and took over. Elliot headed out of the room and waited outside. He wandered down the corridor to a window at the far end that looked out over Lake Placid. The sun was still climbing in the sky over the jagged peaks. He closed his eyes trying to block the noise of those he'd lost in Iraq. Since returning to Lake Placid he'd found writing about his experiences in the army therapeutic. Early in the morning, late at night as the memories flooded in, he would write them down instead of blocking them out. Something about having them on paper allowed him to cope. Before he had pushed them down, carried them into the day and chewed them over as his head hit the pillow. Now he had an outlet, and it was working.

"Elliot. ELLIOT!" Gary said snapping him out of his

dazed state. He turned.

"Yeah?"

He shook his head to indicate that Keith was dead. Gary seemed more disturbed by it than him. He didn't like the idea of a man that had kidnapped a police officer and attempted to kill them hogging medical resources.

"Well I guess we won't get our answer," Elliot said moving past him.

"Is that all you have to say?"

"What do you want me to say, Gary? You want me to mourn for this asshole?"

"I want you to act like a human."

Elliot scoffed. "I'm afraid I lost my humanity in Iraq."

"Bullshit. I was there too, Elliot."

"Oorah!" Elliot said in a mocking tone.

He didn't expand on that but pressed on down the hallway to check in with Officer Jackson.

* * *

Damon awoke that morning to the smell of coffee and toast. For a second he forgot the power had gone out until he pried open his eyes and saw his father holding a piece of bread over a Coleman stove. He and Jesse had slept in the living area while his father had the bed at the far end of the travel trailer. It was surprisingly big inside. He glanced at Jesse who was still sleeping soundly. Damon removed the thick cover and sat up.

"Coffee?" his father asked.

"Yeah. Sure. That sounds good." He pawed at his eyes and slipped his feet back into his boots. Instantly he curled his toes. They were still wet from yesterday. Memories piled on top of one another. Sara alive, dead, the shallow grave, shooting Devin and then almost freezing to death on the way back to Keene.

He gazed around as his father brought over a cup of coffee in a steel mug. "Sorry, there is no milk."

"That's fine."

His father was about five foot nine, medium build and he had a round face. His blond hair was buzzed tight at the side and he had a scar on the right side of his cheek from an ATV crash he'd had when he was a teen. Those in town referred to him by his nickname, Buddy. But he'd always called him Dad.

His father studied him for a second before returning to toasting what looked like moldy bread. Damon stood up and gazed around the trailer. He slipped into the dinette booth and placed his cup on the fold-out table. There were several old newspapers piled up and a to-do list that was partly checked off. His father had always been a stickler for lists. He was organized, something that had come from his years in the army. Unlike Elliot, his father had only given eight years to the military and then left to raise a family. Still all the training and years working for Uncle Sam had left an impression on him.

"So you're in trouble?" his father asked.

"Not exactly."

"Heard you did time."

"From who?"

"Sara. She's a good girl."

"That she was."

He glanced at him. Damon still hadn't told him that

she was dead. When they arrived late last night, both of them were frozen and shivering. He'd spent the first few hours just getting them dry and warmed up. Beyond a few tidbits, conversation mainly revolved around small talk, that was until they both passed out from exhaustion.

"She's dead, Dad."

"What?"

"Magnus shot her."

He stopped toasting bread and dropped it on a plate and brought it over. He slipped into the other side of the dinette and tapped his fingers. "How?"

Over the course of the next twenty minutes he brought him up to speed on what had happened after being released from Rikers, his arrival in Lake Placid, and his confrontation with Cole. When he was done Buddy leaned back and tilted his head.

"Go ahead, I know you're going to say it."

"I told you so."

"Yeah, you did," Damon said. "But everything is hindsight, right?"

"We've all got to find our own way through it." He took a sip of coffee and looked at Jesse. "So you want to go back to Lake Placid and get these two guys to help?"

"It would level the playing field."

"It would. But what if you didn't have to go?"

Damon screwed up his face. "What do you mean?"

"Amos and I can help."

"No, I don't want to get you involved in this. This is on me."

"I want to."

"I can't." He dropped his head. "I appreciate this but I've got to deal with this myself."

"No you don't."

"I do."

His father reached over and placed a hand on his forearm. "You're not my flesh and blood, Damon, but you've always been my kid." He paused. "I know we haven't seen eye to eye but I don't hold a grudge."

"I pushed you out of my life."

"And you had your reasons. Like I said, you don't have

to deal with this by yourself." He cast a glance over to a photo on the counter. It was of his parents, maybe twenty years ago when his mother was alive. "Besides, she would have wanted me to."

He studied his father's face. It was weathered by time and although he was eager to help, he wasn't as fast as he used to be even if he could swear like a sailor and drink anyone under the table.

"You got a vehicle?" Damon asked.

"No but Amos does."

Damon nodded. He didn't know what to say. In all truth he was a little taken aback by the way his father had opened his door to him and welcomed him back in as though the past hadn't happened.

"But I..."

"It's water under the bridge, Damon. Look, there is a good chance none of us are going to survive this winter. Food supplies are dwindling, gasoline for generators is becoming harder to find and violence is on the rise. So the way I see it, today's all we've got and if that means dying." He sniffed hard. "Hell, it's a good day to die."

Damon arched an eyebrow. "Yeah. No offense, but I wanna live."

He burst out laughing. "Oh you thought I meant myself? No. Screw that. I meant them."

Chapter 16

"She's out cold, she won't even know."

Maggie couldn't discern the voice. It faded in and out. As the world slipped into view, her shoulder was in agony. It felt like someone had branded her with a hot iron. And as for the smell, it was rancid like meat that had cooked too long on the BBQ. When her eyes opened, she could make out a black guy looming over her in the process of undoing his pants.

"Dude, she's awake," another voice said.

Blurry images soon snapped into focus and a flood of memories rolled in. Instantly she knew where she was and who was standing before her. "What are you doing?"

Maggie cowered back, and he got on top of her and tried to hold her down.

"Tyron, Cole's coming."

He glanced up then got off her, quickly pulling up his pants. Maggie looked down to see that her jeans had been yanked down to her ankles. They hadn't removed her underwear, but it was clear what they were about to do.

"What the fuck are you doing?" a voice bellowed.

"Cole, we're just having a little fun."

"Yeah? Go jerk off in the bathroom. We're not rapists!" Cole said coming around to the sofa as Maggie quickly pulled up her jeans.

"You know we've got needs."

"And so do I but does that mean I should put a bullet in your head?" Cole said, shoving Tyron away from her. "Now get the hell out of here. Go make yourself useful and rally some people from the town to join us."

"But you said…"

"I changed my mind."

"And if they won't come?"

"Convince them."

Magnus had been sitting nearby watching Tyron and Sawyer.

"Glad to see you've come around to my way of thinking."

"It's not your way. It's mine," Cole said wanting to make it damn clear he was guiding this ship. Magnus got up and headed out with Tyron and Sawyer. They were mumbling something about wanting them out of the picture so he could have her for himself. He looked at Maggie. "You okay?"

She gritted her teeth together and said nothing. What kind of dumb question was that? No, she wasn't okay. She glanced at her wound and grimaced. It was now black and looked like a burnt scab. At least now she knew where the smell was coming from.

"How's the wound?" he asked crouching down like a concerned brother.

Oh this guy was real bright. What was he expecting her to say — thank you?

She furrowed her brow. "I could use something to drink."

"Right."

With the other three gone she figured if there was one chance to escape it was now. He turned but kept his eyes on her as he crossed over to the bar and picked up a bottle of bourbon. "You want alcohol or water?"

"Water, please," she said.

He hopped over the bar and her eyes shifted to the exit then bounced back to him. He glanced beneath the bar and snagged a bottle then vaulted over. She thought he'd have to go into the kitchen, but obviously not.

"Here you go," he said blocking the path of escape. She took it but didn't thank him. There was no way in hell she was going to thank him for anything even if he had prevented his two goons from raping her. She unscrewed the top and chugged it down like she was trying to put out a fire while he took a seat across from her and leaned forward studying her. Once it was empty, she placed it on the table.

"Do you have something to eat?"

He nodded but gave her a skeptical glance.

"I'll see what I can find."

He got up and headed into the rear of the bar and cast a glance at her before disappearing into the kitchen. She waited a few seconds to make sure she could hear him rooting around. "You know, we usually have a chef that makes us everything we want. Can you believe that? The world goes to shit and we still eat like kings."

Maggie eyed the doorway between the bar and the kitchen, then as fast as a flash she bolted for the door. She burst through, her heart catching in her throat as she scanned her surroundings. The tavern was in the middle of nowhere. There were a few houses across the road but that was it. She thrust forward hoping someone, anyone would be in. She cried out as a gust of wind slapped her in the face.

"Help!"

She darted across the parking lot and was climbing up the embankment that led to the main road when a gun went off.

"The next one goes in you!" Cole shouted.

Now maybe she was out of her mind to do what she did next but the way she saw it, she was going to die anyway if she stayed with them and probably get raped.

There was no telling what they had in mind. She squeezed her eyes shut, clenched her jaw and kept running straight across the road. She anticipated the bullet striking her in the back and the same searing pain she'd felt earlier. But it never came. She cast a glance over her shoulder as she sprinted for the nearest home. He was chasing her.

Like a bat out of hell she darted up a gravel driveway. The freezing cold wind cut into her face as she screamed for help. When she made it to the door, she banged hard.

"Open up. Please!"

No answer. She hopped over the porch fencing and circled around back knowing that he was minutes away from catching her. She beat on the rear entrance and even saw someone at the window. Screaming did nothing. She scooped up a yard chair and tossed it at the window in a final desperate attempt to get away from him. It shattered, and she was about to climb in when a man stuck a gun barrel out the window.

"Get back!" the old man bellowed.

Before she could explain, Cole came barreling around the corner with his handgun raised. She cowered back yelling at him to stay away.

"You really are a pain in the ass."

Cole glanced at the man in the window. "Sorry about this. It's the girlfriend's time of the month. What can you do?"

He stuck his gun into his waistband and rushed her. She swung at him and he ducked and scooped her up in a fireman's lift. "Now, now, I know I should have remembered your birthday but there's no need to ruin someone's property. You're so damn selfish."

The old guy inside looked on in utter amazement, completely dumbfounded. He looked more scared than confused or perhaps it was the other way around? Maggie beat on Cole's back while screaming for the man to help but he did nothing.

* * *

Cole lugged her back to the tavern and used his foot to swing open the door. As soon as he had her inside, he tossed her on the floor like a rag doll then turned and stuck a key in the lock and secured it.

"You know, I bring you back here, tend to your wounds, prevent my pals from raping you and even go as far as to get you a drink and prepare you a meal and this is the way you treat me?"

He turned, and she cowered back.

"I have a good mind to teach you some manners myself. Is this how you treat all men?"

"Only the assholes that kidnap."

He chuckled and crossed his arms. "Oh so you think I've kidnapped you?"

"What else do you call it?"

"Leverage. Trading. It doesn't matter what I call it. Believe me, things could be a hell of a lot worse."

She scoffed. "Hardly. Is this how you treat all your friends?"

He walked past her and hopped up onto the bar and pulled out a cigarette. He held out the pack, she shook her head and got up off the floor.

He sniffed as he lit the end of the cigarette. "This world is a different place now."

"Is that how you justify it in your mind?" she shot back.

He scrutinized her as he took a deep drag and exhaled smoke from his nose.

"What's your name?"

She said nothing.

"Come on? What is it?"

"Maggie."

"Huh. Well Maggie. You're not from around here, are you?"

Maggie walked over to the sofa and sat down. Her back was killing her. When he tossed her down, she hit the floor hard. She ran a hand around her back and rubbed it. Since arriving in Keene, she'd felt nothing but pain. "What's that got to do with anything?" she said through gritted teeth.

"City living is a whole different world compared to a small town like this. Where you come from, people don't even look at each other, but here you can't escape people sticking their nose in your business or wanting to give you a hand." He took another drag. "There is a thing called loyalty. Of course you city folk wouldn't know the first thing about it. No, if you don't get your way you resort to lawsuits. You don't think twice about cutting people out of your life. But here, we have a different way of going about things. Sometimes people lose sight of that and they need a little reminder. Damon for instance. You know how long I've known that guy?" he asked.

She pursed her lips and continued rubbing her back.

"Twenty years. Yep. I knew him when were in grade three." He snorted. "We were like this," he said bringing up his hand and crossing his fingers. "I was there when he went through all that crap with his foster family, I was there through the multiple times when Sara dumped his ass."

"And you were there when he took the fall," she said, before quickly adding, "Oh right, I got that wrong. You weren't anywhere to be found." She chuckled.

He narrowed his eyes and pointed at her. "You don't know shit, girl."

"I know you don't throw friends under a bus. What did you expect him to do when he returned? Greet you with open arms? You let your best friend go to jail for eight months."

Cole hopped down, he didn't like anyone accusing him of throwing friends under a bus, or her tone. He ambled over and she backed up expecting him to strike her.

"I don't know what Damon has told you and I know you want to paint me as the bad guy here but you're wrong. What I'm trying to do here is for his good as well as mine."

"Is that why you shot his girlfriend in the back?"

"I didn't do that!" he yelled wanting to make it clear. If he could turn back time, he would have prevented that from happening and by the time this was over, he was going to make damn sure Magnus paid for that.

"Um, doesn't matter, does it? Whatever hope you have

of winning Damon over, is gone. Believe me."

He scoffed. "What, just because you shared a couple of weeks with him, you know him better than I do?"

"Perhaps."

He sneered. "Yeah, right!"

He got up and went over to the bar to get himself a drink. Listening to her crap sober was unbearable. "You have no clue what I'm trying to build here."

"Build? Don't you mean destroy?"

He turned his back to her for a second while he scooped up a bottle of bourbon and returned to his seat. He popped the top off and took a swig before wiping his lips with the back of his sleeve. "If I wanted to destroy, I would have let them rape you. If I wanted to destroy, I would have burnt your eyes out instead of cauterizing your wound. If I wanted to destroy, I would have left your body in a shallow grave in the wilderness. So don't you tell me what I'm trying to do. You have no clue."

"And you do?"

Her comebacks were starting to irritate him.

He took another swig and studied her. She'd been outside in the truck when they'd been questioning Damon about Magnus' cousins. It gave him an idea. He was curious to see if she'd take the bait.

"Alright, there was a reason why we shot his girlfriend."

"Yeah, what?"

"Because he killed two of my friend's cousins in Lake Placid."

Her brow knit together, then she shook her head.

"You're referring to the two lunatics who tried to kill a mother and her two children?"

He played along with it and nodded. "That's right."

She scoffed. "They got what they deserved."

"Magnus would beg to differ."

"Well anyway, it wasn't Damon."

And there it was. He knew he'd eventually figure it out. It was just a matter of time and speaking to the right person. Then it made sense as to why Damon lied to him. He'd told him what he needed to hear so he could get out of the room. That was smart.

"Well it seems Damon is taking the blame. Pity really because he's the one that's had to suffer for it."

She stared back at him and he was waiting for her to fill in the missing piece. The bit about who was behind it. His guess was someone close to the mother and the kids, but who?

"You got it all wrong," Maggie said.

"Really? Then what happened?"

"I just told you. They tried to kill a mother and her two kids."

"So the mother killed them?"

She didn't reply so Cole continued.

"Ah, the protecting the mother." He pointed at her. "I like that. Women sticking together and all that shit."

"She didn't do anything."

"So her kids killed them."

"At their age? No."

"Well that leaves only one person. I'm curious, why did he do it?" Cole had no idea who it was, but he just figured if he pretended to know she might toss a name out and that was all he wanted. A name to give Magnus. He could use that to his benefit. It would regain his confidence and right now he needed that.

"Why do you think? Those animals were attacking his family."

"Ah, I see now. The father. Um. I can appreciate that. If anyone tried to kill my lady or kids, I wouldn't think twice." He frowned purposely. "So if this guy is with your group. Why didn't he tag along?"

"He had better things to do."

"Right. And his name was?" he asked.

C'mon, give it up, he thought. She looked reluctant. It was to be expected. He would just have to try a different approach to getting it out of her.

"So?"

"I'm not telling you."

He laughed. "Oh we're not gonna hurt him. I just wanted to know so when I have a conversation with Damon, I can ask him why he lied?"

"Maybe because he didn't toss him under a bus," Maggie replied.

"Yeah, that's getting real old. So how about you stop dicking me around and give me a name?"

"Fuck you."

Cole brought a hand up to his ear. "What was that? I didn't quite hear you."

"You heard me."

Cole nodded. He was about done with this bitch. In an instant he stood up and pulled the Glock and grabbed a hold of her by the hair and dragged her to the floor as she screamed in agony. He pressed her face down and pushed the barrel of the gun against her temple. "Now I'm only going to ask you one more time. What was his fucking name?"

"Fuck you?"

He chuckled. "Man, I have got to meet this man. To think that Damon and you would cover for him, even risk your lives. He's got to be an important person. I mean he led you out of New York like the Pied Piper of Hamelin.

Now that's the kind of man I'm looking for." He tapped the barrel against her skin. "Last chance!"

He pressed hard on her face making her cry.

Even then she wouldn't say a word.

"Give me a fucking name!"

"Elliot. It's Elliot Wilson."

He waited for a second then released her.

"Good girl. Good." He hauled her up and brought her back to the couch. "See. Now that wasn't so bad, was it?" He grinned before using his thumb to wipe away her tears then bringing it up to his mouth to taste them.

Chapter 17

The Jeep bounced up the curb and Elliot hopped out before killing the engine. His heart was hammering in his chest as he rushed into the house calling out their names. "Rayna. Evan. Lily?"

"What's the matter?" Evan said coming around the corner and almost colliding with him.

He grabbed a hold of him. "Where's your mother?"

Rayna was holding a dishcloth in her hand. "I'm here, Elliot."

"What's up? What happened?"

"Nothing."

His brow furrowed. "What?"

"Nothing's the matter. Why?"

He shifted his weight from one foot to the next. "But I got a message over the radio from Jill saying I needed to head back to the house and talk to you. That it was urgent."

Rayna took a deep breath and closed her eyes.

He could tell something was bothering her. "Rayna, is everything okay?"

"Lily, Evan, can you head upstairs and take Kong with you? I need to chat with your father."

They wandered off, Lily cast a glance over her shoulder and Kong bounded up the stairs. Rayna headed into the kitchen and he followed her in. She went over to the sink where she had a bowl full of water and was in the middle of washing some dishes. She tossed the cloth over her shoulder and leaned back against the counter.

"Why do I get a sense I'm not gonna like this?"

"You need to promise me that you'll listen, and won't lose your cool. I can't have that. The situation is complicated enough as it is. I need you to hear me out."

Elliot nodded. "Whatever it is, it can't be as bad as what I put you through."

He took a seat at the kitchen table and Rayna squeezed her eyes shut then took a deep breath. "How do I put this?" She shook her head as if searching for the words.

She brought a hand up to her face and squeezed the bridge of her nose.

"After you left for New York, I had no idea where you'd gone. No one did. By the evening I phoned Gary to ask if they would search the town because I figured you were suicidal and maybe you'd hurt yourself." She took another breath. "As the days went on and you never returned, I didn't know what to think. I was struggling to cope, wondering if it was my fault. The kids were completely devastated."

Elliot dropped his chin. When he left, he was in a very dark place. Although he had given much thought to how they would cope, he didn't really know how hard it was for them.

"I'm sorry, Rayna."

"You don't need to be. It's in the past. I get it. You were struggling with PTSD and didn't want to put us through it."

"Then what is it?"

"In those first few months after you were gone Gary

and Jill were like my lifeline. I honestly don't think I would have managed if it wasn't for them. They invited us to dinner. They visited often. Gary helped out around the house with odd jobs."

He smiled. That was the one reason why he felt at ease while in New York. He knew they would come to her aid. They were honest, good people and…

As he was thinking that, Rayna started heading down a path that was beginning to sound like something he didn't want to hear.

"Then one thing led to another and…" She blew out her cheeks and looked at him. "I didn't cheat on you while you were away, but Gary came on to me."

Elliot screwed up his face. "What?"

"Like I said. They visited. However, Gary started visiting more often than Jill. He had dinner here one night and had a little too much to drink and made a pass at me."

"And?"

"I pushed him back. Told him I wasn't interested."

He nodded. Good. At least she had stayed faithful. He didn't like it and he was going to have words with Gary for sure, but he understood why Gary might have done it. Rayna was a beautiful woman and long before Gary met Jill, Elliot was aware that he'd liked Rayna. He'd seen the looks he'd given her. The way he changed when he was around her. An attractive woman could do that to a man. As he chewed it over in his mind, he couldn't help wonder why she hadn't told him sooner. Why had it taken a message from Jill to bring up the topic?

"Why didn't you tell me?"

"What do you think? I was scared you'd misunderstand. You've only been back a couple of weeks. I would have eventually told you."

"Would you? Then why did Jill contact me and not you?"

"Isn't it obvious? She's angry at me because she thinks I seduced her husband."

"And why would she think that, if you told her what you've told me?"

Rayna dropped her chin, and he continued.

"What are you not telling me, Rayna? Did you sleep with him?"

"No, but one night I had a little too much to drink, and I didn't push him away when he kissed me. I mean, eventually I did, but I lingered in it."

Elliot tapped his fingers against the table beating out a gentle rhythm.

"Do you feel anything for him?"

"God, no. I told him I didn't want him coming around again unless he was with Jill."

"And has he?"

"No. He's stayed away."

He breathed in deeply and rose to his feet. "I should get going."

"Elliot. I didn't flirt with him. Hell, I didn't even want it to go as far as a kiss. It just happened. Please. Stay."

"I have to go."

"But the kids."

He suddenly realized what she was thinking. He

thumbed over his shoulder. "I told Gary I would meet him at the department."

"So… you're not leaving Lake Placid?"

He chuckled. "No. I promised you I wouldn't leave again, and I meant it."

She got this confused expression on her face. "Aren't you mad?"

He sighed. "Were you, when I returned?"

She shrugged. "I was processing."

"And so am I," he said before turning and walking out. She followed him as he got back into the Jeep.

"Are you going to say anything to Gary?"

"We'll exchange words."

"That's all you'll exchange, though, right?"

Elliot scoffed. "Can't guarantee that."

He fired up the Jeep, and he put it in reverse and started backing out. He looked at her one more time before driving off. She looked worried, but she didn't need to be. The fact was he was surprised she'd even taken him back. Twelve months was a long time to be away, and he had half expected to find her seeing another man, if only because she thought he was dead. He gripped the wheel tightly as he made his way to the town hall. Was he mad? He wouldn't have been human if he didn't feel a little burned by his own friend but in light of what he knew about Gary, he would have been lying to say that the thought of him and Rayna getting close hadn't crossed his mind. At one time he might have blown his top and confronted Gary but that was before New York and before he came to understand the fragility of life.

When he arrived at the town hall he walked in with his mind full of questions.

"Hey Elliot!" Jackson said.

"Please tell me you are not back to your regular duties."

"Hospital released me an hour ago. I don't have anything else to do so I might as well be down here helping out."

"You're a better man than I am," he said jabbing his finger at him. "Where's Gary?"

"In the mayor's office with the chief."

He gave a nod and wandered down the hall. The door was closed but he could hear a heated exchange inside. He gave a knock and Gary opened the door.

"Oh hey Elliot, come on in."

Elliot looked at his old friend through new eyes. There was a part of him that wanted to take a swing and let him know that he knew about his transgression, but he didn't think this was the time or the place. He closed the door behind him. Chief Murphy was sitting in a chair off to the far side with a toothpick in his hand; he gave a nod and turned back to Mayor Hammond.

"Anyway, as I was saying, I think it's important we start to consider new forms of punishment," Ted said.

"Jail isn't enough?" Gary asked.

"Have you seen it lately? It's practically bursting at the seams. We're not set up to handle this level of criminal behavior. Most of these guys would have already been carted off to county by now."

"So we expand it."

"And who's going to monitor them?" Ted asked.

"You. It's not like you're doing anything else around here."

"Watch it. I'm still the chief."

"Assistant," Gary said, quick to correct him.

"Wayland has gone, so the baton has been passed to me."

Gary sneered. "Yeah, isn't that convenient."

Elliot's eyes darted between them. He stood by as an observer while still mulling over what Rayna had told him.

Ted scowled. "I'm not sure I like your tone."

Gary waved him off like he was nothing more than an annoying fly.

"Gentlemen. Please. This isn't getting us anywhere. We are here to discuss how to move forward, and the recent murders."

"We are wasting our time. What is done is done," Ted said, picking at his teeth.

"Ted, please, allow Gary to answer," Hammond said.

"Thank you," Gary said glaring at Ted. He brought him up to speed on what had occurred so far with the return of Jackson, what both he and Elliot had heard outside the home before they raided it and the capture and death of Keith. He then added that he felt that a committee needed to be assigned to make the decisions on who in the community would step into the role of officers.

"We don't need a committee to decide that," Ted said. "I've already compiled a list of those who I believe would be best suited."

"Really? I'd like to see that."

Ted fished out of his internal pocket a folded piece of paper. Gary took it and scanned the list before handing it to Hammond.

"Um, that's interesting. What happened to the list of names from the town hall meeting the other night? I heard there were some good people ready to help."

"They might have been good, but they weren't suited."

"And what criteria are you using to decide that?"

"Don't you worry about it, Gary. We've got this under control."

"Oh I bet you do." He eyed him and the tension in the room thickened.

"Look, it doesn't matter who is helping just as long as we have enough people to man the checkpoints around the town, protect supplies and hunt for food," Hammond added.

"It does matter," Elliot piped up. "You go placing firearms into the wrong hands and you're just asking for trouble."

"That's why I personally compiled this list," Ted said.

"Mind if I take a look?" Elliot asked. The mayor gave it to him and he scanned it while Gary and Red continued to bicker about forms of punishment for those caught stealing, murdering or rape. Elliot handed the list back to Ted.

"Satisfied?" Hammond asked.

He shrugged. "I guess we'll see."

He didn't know them all but the ones he did weren't

known for creating trouble in town. They were honest, hard-working folk who either had some military training or were avid hunters.

"Are they aware there will be no perks for helping?" Gary asked.

"Yes and no," Ted said. "Those who are going to hunt for food, like James Bolton and his pals, are going to want a larger cut."

"Well that's not going to happen," Gary said immediately.

"It will if you want to eat."

"We'll find our own food," Elliot said.

"Not around these parts you won't," Ted replied. "We can't just have anyone out there killing wildlife otherwise we'll run into the same situation of dwindling supplies."

Elliot chuckled and shook his head.

"Something amusing?"

"Yeah. You've got big ideas but not enough people to enforce them. Hell, you can't even deal with the situation in your own backyard."

Ted scowled. "First, we will do whatever is required, second, why are you even in here?"

"Because I invited him," Gary said. "While you've been agonizing over this list, we've actually been out there risking our necks."

Hammond cleared his throat and leaned forward. "Ted, he does raise a valid point. We're not going to be able to stop people from hunting and trapping."

"We will if they want to remain residents of Lake Placid."

Gary turned to him. "I'm sorry but I can't keep a straight face while you're talking. Are you implying that you will kick them out of town if they don't abide by your rules of hunting?"

"Like I said. We need to look at new forms of punishment. And until help shows—"

"Help isn't going to show," Elliot said.

Ted ignored him like he wasn't even in the room. "Until help shows we are still the law in this town and that means we will do whatever is necessary to uphold it."

Gary chuckled. "Well then, let's hear it. What are your ideas for this new form of punishment?"

"It will be judged on a case-by-case basis."

"Well surely you've given it some thought?" Gary was having a dig at him.

He shook his head and looked back at the mayor. "All I'm saying is that in order for us to survive, we need to make some hard decisions. There are only so many mouths we can feed."

"That's why it's important folks should be allowed to hunt," Elliot added.

"Yeah? And what happens when you get one family who decides to kill more than their share? Huh? Sure they will be fine but what about the family that doesn't hunt?"

"So we teach them," Elliot replied.

"It's not happening. Once I have these men and women as officers the first order of business is to remove anyone who is not from the town of Lake Placid."

"You can't do that."

"I can and I will. It's no different from what we are

doing already at the blockades. We are preventing anyone from outside coming in and adding to the strain we are under. Now folks who are not from this town, I'm speaking about tourists or out-of-town family, have a home somewhere. We'll give them enough food and then send them on their way."

"You are going to incite a riot," Gary said.

"That's why my list is important. We'll be ready."

Gary shook his head and put a hand on his hip. "This is bullshit."

"It's only bullshit because you're not calling the shots," he replied. "And if you were, we'd be in a worse state."

"Yeah? How so?"

"I'm not even going to dignify that with a response. It's probably best you stay out of this," Ted replied.

Gary walked over to him and Ted stood up.

"You better stand down," Ted said.

"Or what?"

Hammond raised a hand. "Okay, okay, let's not blow this out of proportion."

Elliot tugged at Gary's arm to get him to drop it. There was no point getting into a fight. It would have only given Ted a reason to cause further trouble later. The tension between them was already close to exploding.

"No, I'd be interested in knowing what you expected me to do with Keith."

"It's pretty obvious. He kidnapped a member of the department."

"Are you suggesting that I should have killed him?"

Ted stared back at him then looked at Hammond. "We are living in different days now. We don't have the manpower to look after criminals and we certainly aren't going to release them."

He wouldn't come out with it and say it, but it was pretty clear what his new forms of punishment would include. Now as much as Elliot didn't agree with him on certain points related to hunting, he was all for disposing of those who could and would threaten the survival of residents.

Mayor Hammond sighed and put his head in his

hand. "Unfortunately, Gary, Ted has a point. We just don't have the manpower to watch over criminals and if we release them, we could be placing the lives of others in jeopardy."

"You're out of your mind," Gary said. "We are not animals."

He glanced at Elliot. "Tell them, Elliot. Tell them that this is not how we do things."

Gary was expecting him to back him up, but he couldn't. It wasn't because of what Rayna had told him or that he even liked Ted. It was common sense and common sense had to be the guiding factor in making decisions. When he didn't respond, Gary looked at him and shook his head. "No. This is not right. I say we bring this decision to a group. And they can be the ones that make that decision."

Hammond tapped his cigar ash in a tray in front of him and leaned forward.

"We did," Hammond said. "You're looking at it."

Chapter 18

When Magnus and the others returned, Cole was pleasantly surprised to see they weren't alone. There was a group of six with them, of course he assumed they weren't there of their own accord. The door swung open and men and women streamed into the room. Ages varied from late teens to mid-thirties. A mixed rabble who looked curious.

"Welcome. Welcome. Welcome," Cole said greeting them like he was about to give a presentation. Behind them Sawyer, Tyron and Magnus walked in. Magnus was quick to make his point.

"See. I told you my way works."

Cole wasn't going to have a pissing match with him. Time was of the essence and now that he had an audience, he planned on playing to it. But before doing so, he shared with Magnus what Maggie had told him.

Magnus scoffed. "Well, I'll be. You found out?"

"Yep. It just requires the right kind of persuasion."

He eyed all three of them. This was what he needed. Something to gain their trust back and let them see that following him made sense. It was a straight-up power play.

"So who was it?"

Cole sniffed. "A man by the name of Elliot Wilson. He lives on the same street as your cousins. He was defending his family."

Magnus was speechless. His mouth turned at the corner.

Satisfied that he'd earned their respect again, Cole hopped up onto the bar eyeing Maggie across the room with a look of glee. This was all working out perfectly. Twelve people weren't a lot, but it was a start and he was confident others would soon join them.

"Ladies and gentlemen. You're probably wondering why you are here. It's very simple. We are living in dangerous times. Unfortunately no one is coming to save you or me. We are on our own. Now you might be thinking that you can survive this by yourself, and you would be wrong. The only way we are going to make it through this is by joining together." He jumped down and walked over to a man in his early twenties. He was thin and looked like he had an attitude. He got real close to his face. "Think about what it would be like to have someone watching your back, someone looking out for your best interests, someone willing to fight to ensure you stay alive. Think about never having to worry about where your next meal is going to come from, or whether you are going to be alive, a day, a month or a year from now. These are just some of the perks of aligning yourselves with us. Together we will not just survive, we will thrive, but it comes at a cost and you must ask yourself, am I willing to pay the cost?" He got almost nose-to-nose with the kid. "Are you?"

Whatever attitude he had vanished, and he nodded.

"Good. Because our fight for survival starts today."

Cole was about to return to his podium on the bar when he turned right into the blade. Magnus offered back a cold stare as he thrust it deeper into his abdomen. Cole clamped on to his leather jacket, gripping him tightly, words unable to escape his lips.

"Why? You're probably wondering why?" Magnus said while the crowd looked on. "It's simple. It just requires the right kind of persuasion," he said, tossing Cole's words back in his face. "People follow that which they fear. Look around you. I did this. Not you. And as long as you are calling the shots we aren't going to survive." He left the blade in and Cole gasped as Magnus pushed him back and Cole dropped to the floor clutching his wound. He cast his gaze to Sawyer and Tyron, but they looked on unsympathetically. Magnus dropped down and relieved him of the handgun in his waistband. "You won't be needing this. You know, Cole, it's been one hell of a ride but if there is anything this shit storm has taught me, it's that all good things come to an end." He took a deep breath and looked up at the crowd of faces. He had their full attention. "I appreciate you extracting that information from her, it saves me a lot of time. Well, I would love to stay and have one last drink but we have work to do. As you so eloquently put it — our survival starts today."

* * *

Amos Jones was an odd-looking fellow. He shuffled around his home in a pair of slippers and a striped robe, and beneath that he wore military fatigues. He was in his early fifties, bald and missing one of his front teeth. Damon's father had spent the better part of two hours trying to convince Amos to let him use his vintage 1949 Caddy. Apparently it was locked up in his garage and rarely saw the light of day even when the country had power. He referred to it as his baby.

Although Buddy was on onboard with helping them, Amos wasn't.

"We'll have it back by the end of the day," Buddy said.

"Famous last words," he replied before taking a hard pull on his oversized cigar. "No, it's probably best you all keep your distance. These kinds of things never work out in the end."

"A girl's life is at stake," Buddy replied.

"And so is my Caddy. You know how many miles that has on it?"

Buddy shook his head

"56,021. That's right, that beauty is a well-oiled machine that is going to net me a tidy profit once I retire."

"Retire? Old man, you'll be lucky to make it till next year," Damon said.

Amos jabbed his finger at him. "You youngsters have no manners. In my day, I would have been whipped with a belt and had my mouth washed out with soap for speaking to my elders that way."

"Oh, come on, let's leave this asshole. We are wasting our time," Jesse said pulling Damon away. "She could be dead by now."

"I just told you. He won't kill her."

"Yeah, well I'm not waiting around for some old coot to find his balls."

Jesse stormed out of the house and Damon took off after him while Buddy continued to work Amos. He'd told them it wasn't going to be easy. Amos was a breed of his own, a recluse who had zero tolerance for anyone that didn't think the same as him. Outside Jesse returned to the trailer to collect his AR-15.

"Give him time. He'll work him down."

"Damon, we don't have time. We are out of it. Now I'm going whether you're coming or not."

"It's a long walk from here."

"Who cares," Jesse said pushing past him.

"Hold up, Jesse."

Jesse wasn't listening to him. He trudged off heading west on Irish Hill Road. Damon ran a hand over his head and sighed before jogging back to the house and heading in the back door. Now he usually could keep his cool but he'd had about enough of this old man's shit. He pulled the Glock from his waistband, charged past his father and while Amos was bending over to pick up his coffee, he grabbed him and stuck the gun against the side of his head.

"Now listen up, you old bastard, I'm done playing

games. We are taking your vehicle whether you like it or not."

"Damon!" his father yelled.

In an instant, the gun he had pressed against his face was out of his hands and Damon was on the floor with it pointed at him. Amos loomed over him, his eyes narrowed.

"I beg to differ."

For a man of his age, he moved fast. Looks were deceiving. Damon put up both hands while his father tried to talk Amos down from putting a hole in his skull.

"Amos. He doesn't know any better."

"Well that's obvious."

He twisted the gun around and handed it back to Damon, grip first. Slowly Damon took it and Amos pulled him up. "You've got balls, kid, I'll give you that." He studied him for a second before heading over to a cabinet. "I'll take you. But I drive."

"Why did it take you so long to decide?" Buddy asked.

"It's a classic."

He fished out some keys and slipped out of his robe. Next, he disappeared into a back room and returned with an M16 rifle, and a bag over one shoulder.

"Well come on then."

He led them down a hallway and through a door into the connected garage. Inside it was pitch-black. Amos didn't turn on a flashlight but made his way down a series of small wooden steps. He pushed up the garage door and daylight flooded the small space to reveal the shape of a vehicle hidden beneath a cream cover. He grabbed a handful of cover and gave it two large tugs. It slipped off to reveal a mint condition, black, 1949 Cadillac OHV V8. It was quite a sight to behold and certainly not what he expected. He unlocked the door and slipped in, then opened the other side for them. Damon noticed there wasn't any rust. It had all the original headlights, dash and doors. It was a four-speed automatic.

"You get this repainted?" Damon asked.

"No," he said before laughing. "This is the original paint."

"How often do you drive it?"

"I've had it out of this garage three times over the past sixteen years."

"Are you kidding me?"

"Oh I've started it up a few times just to hear the roar of the engine but that's about it." He stuck the key in the ignition and fired it up. "The only thing that has been changed is the battery which I got last year. Not bad, eh?"

Damon shrugged. He just wanted to get moving.

After a slow process of reversing out so he didn't scrape it, he closed his garage and got back in and Damon gave him directions. Jesse hadn't made it far down the road but he was moving at a fast pace when they rolled up beside him.

"You want a lift?"

He looked surprised to see them and Damon popped the door for him. He sighed as he got in. "Took you long enough."

"You youngsters wouldn't have survived in my day. Everything has to be now. You don't have a shred of patience."

* * *

As they got closer to the tavern Damon felt his chest tighten. He knew eventually he'd have to kill Cole and with their history that was going to be hard. Prison had given Damon a lot of time to think. So much had changed between them over the years. They were no longer the kids that spent their time playing video games and getting drunk, they'd both grown into people they didn't want to be. The need for money changed things. It had changed them and led them down a destructive path.

Amos veered over to the edge of the road about a hundred yards from the tavern.

"There's no Scout outside. You think they're still in there?" Buddy asked. "Anywhere else they might have gone?"

Damon pushed the door open. "It's possible they went back to the garage but... listen, stay here. I'll go and check it out."

"Not by yourself you aren't," Jesse said.

"We'll remain here," Amos said, tapping his steering wheel. His father agreed. They were both at an age where risking their lives wasn't something they were ready to do — especially for a stranger. Damon and Jesse double-timed it across the road, down a grassy embankment, and pushed their way through some trees to come up around the back of the tavern. He brought up his rifle and approached at a crouch, scanning his surroundings as Jesse watched his six. At the rear of the tavern he peered through a dirty pane of glass into the kitchen. There was no one there. He cupped a hand over his eyes and squinted trying to make out the restaurant area through the doorway. It was too dark to see.

"Anything?"

He shook his head and with two fingers gestured for them to work their way around. They moved quietly staying low to the ground just in case anyone looked out the window. At the side door entrance, he cut a glance through the window but saw no one inside.

"Listen, open the door and I'll head in."

"Are you sure about this?"

"No, but we have no other option. I don't see anyone in there."

"Maybe they parked in a different spot and are waiting to ambush us."

"Just do it," Damon said, stepping back from the door and preparing to unleash a flurry of rounds. He leveled the rifle as Jesse gripped the doorknob. He gave a nod and Jesse yanked it open. Damon slipped in raking his rifle. Not even two seconds after, Jesse was through the door to back him up. The fireplace was crackling. There were empty beer bottles on the counter and a few plates of food but no one.

"They must have gone to the garage," Damon said. "Let's go."

He turned to head out when they heard someone call his name in a soft voice. "Damon!"

They both turned toward the bar. When he made his way around, there on the ground clutching a bottle of bourbon was Cole with a blade still stuck in his stomach.

Damon hurried in and dropped down beside him taking in the sight of his old friend.

"Who did this?"

He coughed. "Magnus."

Damn gritted his teeth.

Cole's skin was clammy and a pasty white.

"Where is he?"

"Lake Placid. He's taken Maggie. They're going after Elliot. He has others with him."

Damon looked at Jesse. Cole reached up and grabbed a hold of Damon's hand, clutching it tightly. "Listen to me, Damon." He swallowed hard trying to summon the strength to say a few words. "I'm sorry. I'm sorry for everything. I..."

"It doesn't matter now," Damon said.

"It does. I was wrong. I should have never sent you in to get those drugs. I should have never let you take the fall. I'm sorry."

His eyes welled up and a single tear trickled out the corner of his eye.

Damon dropped his chin and felt his grasp tighten. Although he knew Cole had lost his way, if he was honest, so had he. Life wasn't easy.

"Damon, we should go," Jesse said. He nodded and looked back at Cole who was struggling to breathe.

"You remember that time when we were thirteen, and I stole my old man's gun and that bottle of liquor?" Cole asked.

Damon nodded.

"I wish I could go back to that time."

Life felt carefree and easy back then. It was like they had the whole world at their fingertips. They would spend hours wandering the back roads and countryside, smoking cigarettes and talking about the future. They had heads full of dreams and nothing seemed impossible. Neither of them knew where they'd end up and neither of them could have imagined this.

"Me too," Damon said. Cole's eyelids would close then open as if he was having trouble holding on to life. He gasped a few times then his breathing would return to normal. Even though all manner of shit had gone down between them, he was still his friend, and the closest one he'd had. He remained there for the next five, maybe ten minutes until he bled out and took his final breath.

As he left that tavern that morning, his heart was full of rage.

It wasn't just because he'd lost his girlfriend and his oldest friend but because it should have never happened. None of it.

Chapter 19

"You're worrying about a bunch of nothing," Elliot said leaving the town hall and heading back to the Jeep. "What Murphy wants will never happen." They were off to bring supplies to those manning the checkpoints. In the first few days after they emerged from the bunker Gary had rallied together those who'd offered protection and security before the blackout. At that time those assisting were mainly made up of police officers. Now there were others who were doing it in the hope of being showed preferential treatment. But neither Gary, Ted nor Hammond had made promises. The less they knew about how fragile the remaining infrastructure was, the better.

"You heard him."

"Even if he managed to enlist all of those folks, he still wouldn't have enough to enforce all those laws. Sure, he might be able to kill criminals but evacuate those not from this town? Best of luck with that. This place is full of tourists all year round. How's he going to enforce that while maintaining the checkpoints, looking after supplies and having others hunting? He might have some good ideas but they are idealistic at best."

"Good ideas?" Gary asked jumping into the Jeep. "Why didn't you back me up?"

"Because despite what you think, he's right about the criminal aspect. We don't have room in the jail for the lawless, so if you want to try and run this town, you'll have to start thinking about new forms of punishment that will send a message to anyone else who's considering breaking the law."

"No, there has to be another way."

Elliot fired up the engine. "There isn't, Gary. When we were returning from New York, we met all kinds of people along the way. I'm talking about the desperate, dangerous and depraved. We had no choice but to kill them."

"That's different."

"Is it? How?"

"We have people here willing to help. As long as we maintain a core group of thirty or more people we can handle this town and the situations that arise. We can deal with them in a lawful and fair manner. Killing innocents isn't the solution."

Elliot shook his head. "But we aren't talking about innocent people."

"You know what I mean."

"Actually no, I don't. Look, I know what you're trying to do, Gary. You want to hold on to what remains of society but it's not able to function the way it did before. Within a year people will starve, kill each other or die from sickness. It's already happening. And, that's not even taking into account all the planes that dropped out of the sky, or those who were affected by the initial blast and radiation fallout. Now just as I said to you before, you have two choices. Fend for yourself or fend for others but if you choose to fend for others, you're going to have to make some hard decisions and one of those is who lives and dies. I'm talking about those who are going to put an unnecessary strain on our limited resources. You want to jail criminals? How are you going to feed them? How are you going to deal with sanitation? Huh?"

"Don't be so condescending," Gary shot back as they drove along Station Street heading for the first checkpoint. "I know these things."

"Then you understand that Ted has a point."

"I understand that Ted is going to incite riots."

"That's the cost of trying to control the masses," Elliot shot back. "And none of you are ready for that."

Gary continued to look ahead.

When they arrived at the checkpoint on Station Road and Old Military Road, Elliot hopped out and went around to the rear of the Jeep to bring a small box of canned peaches and potatoes to two armed helpers. One of them was a cop. There were five checkpoints around town, the one here, one on Sentinel Road, another on NY-86, another on Sara-Placid Road, and the final one on Ruissemont Road and Mirror Lake Drive. Each one was manned by two people, one of those two was a cop to ensure that nothing got out of hand. They were all given walkie-talkies, which could be used to communicate with one another and call for assistance. Those checkpoints were to be manned twenty-four hours with three shift rotations taking place — one at eight, another at four, and a third at midnight. Everyone was meant to be involved in that but due to a shortage of people only three of those five checkpoints were being manned at any given time.

"Sergeant," Officer Palmer said stepping up to greet them.

"How's it been?" Gary asked hopping out and getting an update. As Elliot handed over the cans he glanced at Gary. He could see he thrived at continuing to play the role he'd once been so good at. His mind went back to what Rayna had said and even though he was still trying to come to terms with it, he would have been lying to say that he didn't feel resentment and anger toward him.

"We had a group of six people who came up from Averyville that attempted to cause some trouble but it wasn't anything we couldn't handle," Palmer said.

"Good."

"Any chance of swapping out with someone else?" Palmer asked.

"Maybe this afternoon. Murphy has another thirty people that will be helping so that should alleviate some of the stress."

"That's a relief as I was starting to think I couldn't do this anymore."

"What do you mean? This isn't anything compared to what you used to do, Palmer."

Palmer shifted his weight and ran a hand around the back of his neck. "Yeah, when we had vehicles. It's freezing cold out here, we have no shelter and I have been standing on my feet for the past five hours. Have you done this yet?"

"You know that's not my job."

"It's not mine either," he shot back. The guy beside him grumbled.

Gary studied him searching for words. Elliot could tell

this was a sign of the times. First society would unravel, and then what little infrastructure remained would go next. That's why he'd told Gary that he was worrying about a bunch of nothing. At the end of the day they were dealing with people, and it didn't matter what role they had stepped into before all of this. Everyone had their breaking point. These folks weren't getting paid and New York winters were brutal at the best of times. A cold wind hit them and Elliot shivered.

Gary leveled up to him and for a second Elliot thought he was going to come down on the guy, instead he placed a hand on his arm. "Look, I understand your frustration and believe me, we are trying to improve the situation for everyone. Things will get better, Palmer, but we need to work through these initial growing pains as we try to establish some normality. Your mother Joanne, she's at the Olympic Center, correct?"

He nodded.

"If you're questioning why you're doing it. Think about her. Right now you and the others are what stands between them living or dying. If we let our guard down for even a minute, it could have a devastating effect." He then brought him up to speed on what had happened with Jackson and explained that his job was to ensure residents remained safe inside of the town. "We don't have it any easier than you. Now look, I know you're cold and you still have three hours left of your shift, so go and get in the Jeep. Warm yourselves up, have something to eat and we'll take over here for a few minutes, okay?"

Palmer nodded and brushed past him with the volunteer. Elliot observed them hop into the Jeep and fire it up.

"That's going to burn a lot of gas."

"It's worth it," Gary replied. "If these people lose heart, we lose this town and that's all we have right now. Each other."

Elliot pulled a pack of smokes from his pocket and tapped one out. He lit it and stuck his hands in his pockets as the wind nipped at his ears.

"Is that so," Elliot muttered.

Gary shot him a glance.

"What's that supposed to mean?"

"It means you put a lot of trust in people you barely know."

"Well maybe those same people will save your ass one day."

"And maybe they won't. You saw the look in that guy's eyes. I give him two more days out here before he throws the towel in. Mother or not. Everyone has their breaking point including friends."

Gary pulled his jacket around and eyed Elliot.

"Including friends?"

"Yep," Elliot replied.

"Why, you thinking of bailing? Cause look at how that worked out."

Elliot took a hard pull on his cigarette and blew smoke out his nose.

"How did that work out?" Elliot tossed his words back at him.

He shot him a look waiting for a response.

Gary scoffed. "You know."

"Actually no I didn't until earlier today."

"What?"

"You going to look me in the face and lie to me? C'mon, I thought you were better than that."

"Perhaps you need to join them in the Jeep and have a rest," Gary said.

"Oh I'm wide awake. Yep. The question is, are you?"

"I don't have a clue what you're on about, but I wish you would reach the punch line."

There was silence for a minute, then without looking at him Elliot threw it out there. He knew unless he asked him directly he wasn't going to get shit out of him.

"Why did you do it, Gary?"

"Do what?"

"Stop fucking lying. Jill deserves better than this. In fact if it wasn't for her I wouldn't have even known."

His eyes locked on Elliot's and he must have clued in at that moment.

"Look, I don't know what Jill's been telling you, but

she's been under a lot of stress lately with me working all these hours."

"Jill didn't tell me anything. It was Rayna." He scrunched up his face. "You know when I left Lake Placid, I wasn't in the right frame of mind. I admit that. I couldn't be the father or husband that my family needed because of PTSD. The only thing that made sense was to get away, and to not have them see me like that. And you know what?" He paused. "When I was in New York, I got through it because I knew you were there to help them. Yeah. My good friend was there to help out and make sure they were safe."

"Elliot."

"No. You listen to me. I trusted you and you went behind my back."

"You were gone for over a year."

"Oh so that gives you the right to move in on another man's wife? Tell me, Gary, how long did you wait? A week, a month, a year?"

"It just happened."

"Don't give me that shit. You fall over, that just happened, but you come on to my wife — that doesn't just happen. You put her in that situation. You could have walked away. And what about Jill? Huh? Have you stopped for one second to ask how this has affected your wife?"

"Elliot... I don't know what I was thinking."

"No, you did."

"I'm sorry."

Elliot turned and jabbed his finger into his chest. "It's not me you should be saying that to. It's Jill. She's the one that sat by and knew about this and didn't say a damn thing to you. She's the one that hasn't kicked your ass to the curb. She's the one that you should be having this conversation with. Me? I just want to put you on your ass."

Elliot stepped forward pressing up against him. It was taking everything he had to hold back.

Gary threw his hands up. "Go ahead. Go on. I deserve it."

"No." Elliot shook his head. "You're not worth it."

He turned his back to him. In his time away in New York, it had taught him many things, most of which was about what really mattered and not to waste his energy on anything that didn't help him get through another day. Beating the shit out of Gary might have given him personal satisfaction but it wouldn't change things. The truth was if he hadn't left, none of this would have happened. He only had himself to blame.

Right then Gary's radio started to crackle.

"Sarge. Sarge. Come in, it's Jackson."

Gary glanced at Elliot. "Go ahead."

"We've got a problem at the checkpoint on 86. Where are you now?"

"On the west side. What is it?"

"I think it's best you see for yourself."

"Roger that, we'll be there in ten."

He looked at Elliot and before he could say anything he headed for the Jeep.

* * *

On the short journey over to the east checkpoint, Gary said nothing. It felt good to get it out in the open if only to make it clear that whatever had happened was over. A small part of him wondered if Rayna was telling the truth. Had she slept with him? He pushed the thought of it from his mind and tried to focus on what was before them. As they got closer, it became clearer what the problem was. Officer Jackson and a volunteer were standing by a truck, their guns drawn and on the ready as if expecting trouble. Gary eased off the gas and hopped out. As they came around the truck, they saw the bodies of the two individuals who'd been manning that checkpoint.

"What happened?" Elliot was first to ask.

"They were dead when we arrived. Weapons are gone. I'm guessing they were ambushed."

"Shit!" Gary said eyeing the tree line and the road that fed down into a residential area. Cobble Hill Road connected to Northwood and then fed into Mirror Lake Drive.

"Sarge, we need more people. Two people to a checkpoint is not enough," Jackson said as he followed Gary back to the vehicle.

"Gary, give me your radio," Elliot asked.

He handed it to him while they continued to talk. Elliot wanted to check on Rayna and the kids. He walked back to the Jeep, so he was out of earshot. He didn't want Rayna to worry, but he had to be sure his family was safe.

Chapter 20

When Foster Goodman entered the town hall that afternoon he had no doubt in his mind of what needed to be done. He covered the Glock in his waistband and adjusted the rifle slung over his shoulder. If there was a line in the sand, he'd stepped over it and there was no going back. In his mind the only way forward was to finish what he'd started.

He took in his surroundings, having been in the town hall countless times. As he walked the corridor that led into the command center, Foster wasn't surprised by the lack of police presence, or volunteers. Everything they had in the way of resources was now being thrown at the town. They were already overwhelmed and the real chaos hadn't even begun.

As he passed one single armed officer, he gave a nod before entering an empty office full of tables, computers, and plans of the city on the wall. For all their planning they couldn't plan for chaos. It was unpredictable.

His mind flashed back to earlier that morning, and the three individuals — a hunter by the name of James Bolton whose son had been beaten within an inch of his life, Timothy Garret whose daughter had been raped, and Wes Francis whose wife had been murdered a week ago by home invaders.

"So? Why are we here?" James Bolton shrugged as he leaned against a decaying wall. He'd arranged to have them meet at a home on the north side that had been partly destroyed.

Foster shifted his weight from one foot to the next. "We all have something in common. Pain. Loss. Suffering. We all agree that the police and mayor are doing nothing to deal with the situation before us. They are biding their time and trying to give the illusion of control. We've heard their empty promises. We've seen the lack of support and felt abandoned. Now we can continue to place our faith in them or we can do something about it. I say we stand up to them, be the ones to decide how we'll live. James, hunting is a long and arduous game. Shouldn't you receive the lion's share if you're the one whose blood, sweat and tears have been shed?" He nodded. "Timothy. Let me guess, the police aren't even searching for your daughter's rapist?" Timothy dropped his head. "And yet you are the one that is reminded of it every day." He turned his attention to Wes. "And Wes, where were the police when raiders broke into your home and bludgeoned your wife to death?" He gritted his teeth.

"Nowhere," Wes replied.

"Exactly. And yet this was after they had made their promises. This is just the beginning. Our situations are going to get a lot worse. You've seen the dwindling supplies in the Olympic Center. You've seen the inability of the police to control and protect. And yet you still see the way they are trying to control us. Everything you heard at that town hall meeting beyond the problems they are facing is a lie. They don't have a solution for food, they don't have a solution for protecting us, and they certainly have no idea of how to govern. Meanwhile, raiders continue to kill, rape and take whatever they want."

"What are you suggesting?" James asked.

"I'm not suggesting anything. I'm here to listen to you all."

Foster knew that the biggest problem facing the town was not a lack of ideas to improve the situation, it was that no one was listening. At first he thought it would be easy to pay off tweakers to raise a little hell, but they had screwed up and kidnapped a police officer. No, the way forward was to use those who had a need for justice and being as the cops weren't able to give them that, perhaps he could.

"Yeah thanks, but I'm not into therapy sessions," Wes said getting up to leave.

"Wes, do you want to punish those who killed your wife?"

He turned, his face a mask of pain. "Of course I do but I'd need to find them and even if I did, I would be outnumbered."

"Not if you have us beside you."

"And what about the police?"

"Minor details."

James Bolton laughed. "Minor. Please. They're the ones

running the show."

"It's all smoke and mirrors, James. You've heard what they want you to hear. I've heard what they don't want you to hear. The department is barely hanging on by a thread. There is internal bickering. The few officers that are still operating are growing tired. Give it another week, two at the most and even they will abandon their post. What then? Huh? Chief Wayland is already dead, and Murphy, he's on the way out."

"Well until he is, I don't see things changing," Timothy said shaking his head and folding his arms.

Foster jabbed his finger at the ground. "So then we have to change it."

"And how do you suggest we do that?"

"Like I told you, I'm not suggesting anything. I'm here to listen to you all. How do you think it should change?"

Foster had realized that asking them how they would want to move forward was what the police and mayor weren't doing. They were telling them how things were going to be, they were deciding where food would go, and they were the ones trying to infringe on their God-given rights.

"Rumor has it, they are considering confiscating guns as a first step to control the violence. You know what happens if we let them do that? Anarchy. How will you protect yourself? How will you hunt for food? How will you prevent them from telling you what you must do?"

Foster hadn't heard them say it yet, but he assumed it was on the horizon.

"The second amendment says it's our right to keep and bear arms, and it shall not be infringed."

"Who told you the cops were going to confiscate?" James asked.

"A volunteer down at the department. Plans are being drawn up as we speak."

James scoffed. "No one is stripping me of my gun."

"And so they shouldn't," he replied.

There was silence for a minute or two. Foster wanted them to chew it over. He could see the look of anger in their expressions. This was exactly what he wanted. The fact was when their world was teetering on the edge of an abyss it didn't take much to push someone over.

"You must have some idea of what you want?" James asked.

"I do but you might not like it," Foster replied.

They looked at one another feeding off each other's negative energy. Foster smiled.

"Tell us."

Suffering had a way of causing even the most level-headed people to lose sight of their morals.

Foster snapped back into the moment as he approached the office of Assistant Chief Ted Murphy. He gave the door a knock and looked behind him to see if the officer he'd passed was going to be a problem.

"Come in."

Foster entered.

"Ah Foster, what can I do for you?"

He closed the door behind him.

* * *

Rayna sat in Jill's kitchen with a hot cup of coffee in her lap while Kong and the kids dashed around in the backyard. Though it was cold, it didn't seem to bother them. Jill took a seat across from her. Her lips pursed, and she held her head high as if knowing what she was about to say.

"I understand what you did. I mean, contacting Elliot."

"He needed to know."

"I agree."

"So?"

"I told him. Everything." She breathed in deeply and took a sip of her drink. "I don't know how he's dealing with it but he knows."

"Good," she said without hesitation.

"And have you spoken with Gary?"

"Not yet."

Her answers were short and to the point as if she wanted to avoid small talk. Rayna gazed around the kitchen and thought about all the times she'd had dinner there. The nights of wine and laughter, the tears they'd shared and the comfort they'd found in each other as wives of ex-military personnel.

"Are you planning on leaving him?" Rayna asked.

"Why would I?" Her eyebrows rose. "It wasn't his fault."

Rayna's brow furrowed. "You still believe I seduced him, don't you?"

"I know you did."

"After all this time you think I would deliberately do something to hurt you?"

She took a sip of her drink and looked away uninterested in replying. Rayna shook her head. She understood the world was falling apart, but she didn't think her relationships would. Jill didn't want to admit that her husband who she adored would show any affection toward anyone else but her. Who would admit that? If she could have blamed it on the alcohol that might have been easier to swallow but Gary had made advances even when he wasn't drinking.

"I'm sorry you feel that way. You must think very little of me if you think I would do that. I expected more from you."

"More from me?" Jill said turning toward her, her tone full of venom.

"You're my best friend, Jill."

"I was until this."

She shook her head unsure of what else would convince her. It wasn't even worth having the conversation. She'd already made up her mind and wasn't budging. Rayna looked toward her children and finished up her drink. Just being around her was uncomfortable. She thought she could resolve it by coming over and letting her know that she'd spoken with Elliot and by telling her the truth but what was the point? She had blinders on. Rayna got up and called to the kids. "Let's go."

* * *

Getting no answer on the radio, Elliot handed it back to Gary who was in the process of checking out the tree line just in case whoever had done this had retreated into the surrounding forest. Nearby, Jackson had a radio up to one ear and a finger in the other.

"Oldman, speak up, I can barely hear you."

His voice kept crackling over the radio.

"There is a riot."

"A riot?" He looked at Elliot. "Sarge! We've got problems."

He continued speaking to Officer Oldman as he made his way over.

"An officer is down, and a riot has erupted at the Olympic Center."

"Well get Palmer or one of the others over there."

"He's the one that's down."

"What?"

Gary snatched up the radio. "Oldman, what is going on?"

Static came over the line and his voice kept cutting in and out. In the background they could hear people shouting and guns firing. "Sarge, we need backup!"

Without wasting a moment they hurried over to the Jeep and hopped in, Jackson followed in a battered old truck that was barely functioning. As one of the first orders of business after emerging from twelve days inside the bunker, Gary and the other officers handed out flyers requesting any vehicle that was operational to be made known. There weren't many, so some of the police and volunteers had to be dropped off at checkpoints.

After getting in the Jeep, Gary smashed the accelerator and tore out of there with Jackson not far behind.

* * *

Magnus shattered one of the rear windows on the home before climbing inside. Sawyer and Tyron joined him while the other six remained outside keeping an eye out for possible threats. He couldn't understand what Cole's problem was. It was easy to control them. Before leaving the tavern, he'd fed them and given them alcohol to lower their inhibitions. Though Sawyer was nervous about arming them so soon after gathering them together, he'd reassured him that they had nothing to worry about. They'd already given them more than anyone else had in town. He'd also used wisdom and approached six individuals he knew either personally or indirectly through other friends, people who were struggling and were looking for hope.

That's what he offered them now — hope of a new tomorrow.

Tyron held Maggie tightly and dragged her around like she was a rag doll. Magnus walked over to the mantelpiece and picked up a photo of the happy family. It was a shot of them standing beside Elliot in full uniform.

"Interesting. Seems we got ourselves a military boy," Magnus said before dropping the photo and crunching the glass below his boot. "Oh well, they bleed just the same." He swiped his hand across the surface of the mantel knocking flowers, photo frames and décor to the floor. It clattered, and some of the ceramic cracked.

"Well make yourselves comfy, boys. We'll wait until he returns and give the man a hero's welcome."

Magnus strolled over to the window and hollered out. "Come on in, guys."

He believed as long as he treated them with respect and showed them at every step of the way that he was in control, they'd fall in line. Killing Cole had been in the cards for years. If the power grid hadn't gone down, Cole would have still died. His lack of judgment in business, his inability to make the hard choices made him weak. Magnus could smell it. He wasn't the same guy he was when Magnus first met him. And after the way he treated Damon, he knew it was only a matter of time before he got them in trouble with the law or worse — killed. Nope, he wasn't going to find himself on the end of a bullet or stuck behind bars because of Cole. The future was his for the taking and he damn well was going to make sure it worked in his favor.

Once Elliot was dead, he'd return to Keene and set in motion a new way of living, one in which those who worked with him would live and anyone who refused or resisted would be killed. It wouldn't take long for people to get in line. Either they helped, or they were of no use to him. He'd set up checkpoints; gather together a group that was fifty strong and then branch out into smaller towns in the area, draining them of their resources. It wouldn't take long to establish themselves as a group to be feared. As for those who would try to knock him off his game, it wouldn't end well. He would keep a group around him at all times just in case anyone wanted to challenge his authority.

He strolled into the kitchen and began going through the cupboards. "Where's he keep his food?"

"I don't know," Maggie said.

Magnus grinned and walked over to her and grabbed her by the ear, bringing her head down to chest level. "Bitch, don't play with me. Where is it?"

She let out a cry like a stuck pig. "Down in the bunker."

Maggie motioned with her head toward the yard.

"A bunker? Huh, well how about that? Maybe Trent wasn't a fool after all." He pulled Maggie away from Tyron's grasp and led her to the back door, tossing her outside. "Lead the way."

Chapter 21

It was complete pandemonium. When they arrived Officer Oldman was outside waiting to meet them. He'd taken cover behind a truck and was getting assistance from two volunteers who were both armed. Gary swerved the Jeep in behind his vehicle and hurried over. Jackson pulled in close behind them to create a barrier.

"What's going on?" Gary asked.

"James Bolton, and another man I can't recognize entered about forty minutes ago. They instructed everyone to get out if they wanted to live. They shot Palmer who was visiting his mother at the time. They've barricaded themselves in there."

Gary frowned. "And where the hell were you?"

"In the vehicle taking my lunch break."

"You've got to be joking?"

"Sarge, I have to eat."

"So no one did anything?" He looked at the two

volunteers who looked scared shitless. They shrugged. And right there was the reason why making people officers wouldn't have worked. Wearing a badge meant nothing without training. The inability to think on their feet meant when the shit hit the fan they would choose self-preservation over all things. Whereas officers and soldiers were trained to face their fears and ultimately do their job, even if it meant losing their life in the process. Elliot scooted up to the corner of the truck with his AR-15 in hand and peered around. The Olympic Center was a huge, three-story, gray brick building with lots of tinted windows. It made it hard to see the suspects. There were two tiers of balconies that might offer them a way to get in unnoticed and a possibility of entry via the side but without being able to see them they would be taking a big risk. Elliot pulled back.

"Are you sure it's just two?" he asked.

Oldman nodded.

"Have you asked him what he wants?" Gary asked.

"I didn't have a chance. The few attempts I've made to

get close I've come under heavy fire."

"From where?"

"They keep shifting position."

"Fuck!" Gary said.

"But that isn't the worst of it."

Gary rolled his eyes. "How can this get any worse?"

"I just heard from two of our officers that a number of fires have been started on the north and east side. Fourteen homes have already been wiped out, the hardware store and a pharmacy are engulfed in flames and even with all this snow, it's still burning out of control."

Gary peered through the passenger side window. "Two individuals storm our main supply area, fires break out. Oh no, not a coincidence at all. Bastards. I wouldn't be surprised if Murphy is behind this."

"The chief?" Oldman asked.

"Assistant."

"You don't know that, Gary," Elliot said taking another look.

"You heard him. What better way to get the

townspeople behind him in executing criminals than to create his own form of chaos?"

"It doesn't matter. Right now, we need to gain control of that building again. I have an idea." He shuffled over and pointed to Olympic Road that ran northeast of the building. "There is a low balcony on the east side. Oldman, I want you to take your truck and drive it at the main doors. Jackson, you and the others will provide cover from here. No doubt they're watching. While you do that, we'll go around the side and breach the east."

"You want me to what?" Oldman asked. "Hell no, they've already killed one cop."

"We don't have any other choice. We need to get inside and end this now."

He looked reluctant, but that was to be expected. They were all going beyond the call of duty. Oldman popped open the passenger side and slipped in while Gary and Elliot returned to the Jeep and reversed back up Main Street and brought the Jeep around into the parking lot of the Crowne Plaza. As soon as Oldman hit the building, they would drive up to the east side, get out, hop on the roof of the Jeep and climb up.

"We'll need to move fast. I'll climb, you watch my six," Elliot said as he revved the engine waiting for Oldman to make his move. A few seconds, then a minute passed.

"What is he waiting for?" Gary asked with a scowl on his face.

"The guy's scared."

"Aren't we all?"

Elliot cast him a sideways glance. Right then Oldman hit the gas and the truck lunged forward. It went up the curb and then came the gunfire.

"Go!" Gary yelled. Elliot smashed the accelerator and tore around to the side of the building. He ducked as he got out after hearing steady gunfire. At first he couldn't tell if they were coming under attack or if it was Oldman. He gave it ten seconds before he scrambled up like a monkey. Gary followed suit, and he reached for Elliot's hand. As he latched on to it, for a split second a thought of letting go went through Elliot's mind. It didn't last. Once over, Gary used the butt of his rifle to shatter a pane of glass and they climbed into a conference room. There was a large mahogany table that seated twenty people and black leather chairs. They hurried past it and exited the door and entered the carpeted corridor. They could hear gunfire as they hugged the wall with their backs and headed in the direction of all the commotion.

* * *

"You know this is like *Driving Miss Daisy*. Can't you go any faster?" Jesse asked. The damn car hadn't gone over 55 mph since leaving Keene. They were crawling along.

"No can do! I'm not getting this paint chipped. This is the original."

"This guy is out of his mind," Jesse said, turning to Damon who hadn't said a word since leaving the tavern. Jesse studied his face. The look of anguish hadn't changed. "You know Cole would have killed us in that forest."

"He was still a good friend of mine."

"You certainly know how to pick friends," Jesse replied. They were just coming up to the turnoff for Cobble Hill Road when they saw the dead officer and volunteer near the checkpoint. Amos brought the vehicle to a stop. It idled as Jesse jumped out to check on them. Damon wanted to keep going but he wouldn't leave without first making sure they were dead. One glance and that was enough. He didn't even have to touch their pulse. Their bodies were riddled with bullets and the surrounding snow was soaked in blood. After returning to the vehicle they veered onto Cobble Hill Road.

* * *

Rayna held back tears as she strolled up Mirror Lake Drive thinking about her conversation with Jill. She was exhausted and tired of having to explain herself. The fact that Gary hadn't said anything to her only infuriated her more. A cold wind blew hard causing snowdrifts against the corners of homes and cars. She kept a tight grip on Kong's leash as they headed back home. Evan and Lily were bundled up with so many layers they could barely walk. She passed several neighbors carrying rifles. It was becoming the norm as people lived in fear of home invaders. After what had occurred two weeks ago, word had spread fast and everyone she knew was taking some form of precaution — whether that was leaving their homes and staying at the Olympic Center or moving in with neighbors to double their chances of survival.

* * *

Elliot moved along the corridors raking his gun and fully expecting to engage with a suspect at any second. His heart was pounding in his chest, beads of sweat formed on his brow and he could hear the blood rushing in his ears.

From the second level they could see Oldman reverse his vehicle in a haphazard manner. The windshield and metal were riddled with bullets and steam was rising from holes in the hood.

They entered the stairwell, and he held the door as Gary took the lead. The closer they got to the first floor they could hear voices echoing and rifles being reloaded.

"They're not getting in, don't worry," a gruff male voice said.

At the door to the next level Gary cracked it open and Elliot took a look. He could only see one way down the corridor and no one was there which meant they were either farther down or to the right. They waited ten, maybe twenty seconds until they heard more gunfire before Elliot gave a nod to Gary to pull the door. He would go left while Gary went right. Elliot tossed up three fingers and counted down. As soon as he hit one, they moved out. There was no one to the left. It was a long corridor with plush carpet and multiple thick pillars. Both men had positioned themselves in an area by the window on the west side of the building. There was about sixty yards between them and the suspects. Both were dressed in hunting gear. One looked in his direction and shouted.

Before he could raise his rifle, Elliot took the shot, sending the man staggering back. Gary trained his rifle on the second guy and dropped him with two shots to the chest. They quickly took cover behind pillars as three rounds punched through drywall and glass, sending shards across the room.

James Bolton kept them under steady gunfire as he staggered away taking cover behind pillars before ducking into a stairwell farther down. The thud of the door got them moving. They hustled down the corridor and made it to the exit. Gary kicked the door open and pulled back as rapid fire peppered the walls on the other side. Elliot could hear him breathing hard and groaning. He wasn't sure where he'd struck him, but he was injured badly and chances of him escaping were getting slimmer by the second. Elliot entered the stairwell hugging the wall and moving down the staircase as Gary fired a few rounds between the steps.

On the way down they saw blood smeared against the wall where Bolton had obviously used it for support. When they reached the ground and emerged, Bolton turned but he was out of ammo. As he tried to load another magazine in, Elliot fired a bullet in his leg. He crashed to the ground with a thud and screamed in agony clutching his thigh as they hurried over. Gary kicked his weapon out of the way while Elliot dropped down and grabbed him by the collar.

"Who put you up to this? Huh?"

"Fuck you."

Elliot stood up and pressed his boot down on Bolton's wound. He screamed.

"Give me a name!"

It was possible that no one had, and they were simply acting out of desperation and greed, but neither he nor Gary could ignore the timing of the sudden surge in fires across the town. Gary stepped in. "Elliot!"

He shook him off. "No, I want a name!"

Bolton's mouth opened, letting out an ear-piercing scream before he gave up the name. "Foster Goodman. It was Goodman!"

Elliot released his foot and before Gary had a chance to intervene, he withdrew his Glock and fired a single round into Bolton's skull. He felt a tinge of satisfaction as he holstered.

"Goodman?" Gary said. "But…"

Elliot didn't linger to discuss it, he was already on his way out the door when Gary caught up with him. "He's behind this?"

"Why does that surprise you?"

"Because he's been helping us."

"And? You've heard the term green on blue. This is no different."

Green on blue was a term used when Afghan soldiers attacked the U.S. Army. These were the same allied forces that were meant to be helping. Why? People could give any number of reasons why. In this case, it was obvious. Most locals had read the news about the crash two years ago and the accusations thrown at the department by Goodman and others.

As soon as they were outside, Gary got on the radio broadcasting a message to the remaining officers and volunteers to be on the lookout for Foster Goodman.

"You are to approach with caution. I repeat. Consider him armed and dangerous."

* * *

Maggie was a wreck. She felt terrible both physically and emotionally. She wished she hadn't told Cole about Elliot but after witnessing his men kill Sara, she thought he'd do the same to her. Now she watched helplessly as they dragged all of Elliot's supplies out of the bunker — bags of sugar, rice, salt, canned goods, beans, coffee, jerky, dried fruits, packaged meals like MREs, granola bars and trail mix along with medication, multivitamins and comfort foods. They'd worked their way through a lot in two weeks but there was ample remaining.

Magnus acted like a supervisor telling them where to stack it. He had a cigarette in the corner of his mouth and one leg up on a picnic table.

"That's it, just put them at the back there, we'll take them when we leave."

Sawyer held a firm grip on the back of her collar and would tap her cheek occasionally with the barrel of his gun just to let her know not to try anything. They hadn't let her out of their sight since Keene. Tyron came over sweating and crouched down in front of her. "Once this is over, I'm going to finish what I started." He wiped sweat from his brow and ran it across her lip. She spat in his face and in an instant he lashed out with a backhand. Her face jerked to the side, and she felt her skin sting.

"Hey!" Magnus said pointing over at them. "There will be plenty of time for that later. Keep hauling that shit out." Tyron wagged his finger in Maggie's face and got real close.

"Your ass is mine."

He walked off grinning and joined the others. The rest of them were like him, completely blind followers not questioning Magnus. She wiped blood from her lip as she remained in a kneeling position.

"So are you like him?" Maggie asked.

"Shut it."

"Well? Are you?"

"You really should keep your mouth shut."

"Man, it must suck being someone else's bitch," she said to Sawyer.

"Well you'll know soon enough," he retorted. "Now shut up!"

"Or what? You're all gonna be dead before the day's out, anyway. Just like his cousins."

Sawyer crouched down beside her and she eyed the blade in the sheath around his calf. It was snapped shut with a button so the chances of being able to go for it and escape were slim to none but that didn't mean she couldn't try something.

"Lady, the only one who was protecting you before this was Cole, and he's gone. So I recommend choosing your words wisely."

"Oh, I'm just having some fun with you," she said turning and rubbing her hand up between his legs. He got this smile on his face and nodded slowly. Then just as she was about to wrap her fingers around the blade, his hand clamped down on hers squeezing it tight. She let out a groan, and he pushed her hand away.

"Nice try."

Right then one of Magnus' men came hurrying out the back of the house. "Magnus. We got company."

Chapter 22

"Rayna? Are you there?"

Magnus held tightly to Maggie's arm and pressed a Glock into her rib cage to remind her of what would happen if she screwed up. Maggie peered through the peephole. She recognized him by his voice, but she wanted to see if he was alone. Everything inside her wanted to scream for him to run but that wouldn't end well.

"Who is it?" Magnus asked in a hushed tone.

"Mr. Thompson. He's a neighbor."

"Get rid of him." He pressed the muzzle harder against her rib cage. "You say anything, you blink or even make a gesture, I'll kill you and then him. You understand?"

She nodded. He positioned himself behind the solid oak door as she went through the process of dealing with the multiple locks. She pulled the door open just slightly.

"Oh hey Maggie, I'm just returning that lantern I

borrowed. Is Rayna or Elliot in?"

She gave a strained smile. "Actually, they're out at the moment but I'll give it to them." She reached forward and grasped it but he didn't release it.

His brow furrowed. "Everything okay?"

"Yeah. Yeah. Just tired. Hungry. You know how it is."

"Right." He nodded slowly. "So Kong not around?"

"No, he went with Rayna."

"To where?"

"Um. Not sure. I think it might have been the town hall."

"Alright. Anything you need a hand with?"

Maggie felt Magnus tighten his grip on her.

"That's very kind of you but no. We are good. I'll speak to you later, okay? Say hello to your son for me."

"My... Oh, yeah, huh, I'll do that."

She closed the door and Magnus looked through the peephole. "Go on, old man. Leave," he muttered in a low voice. He stayed there looking through the peephole and then turned back toward Maggie and scowled. Something wasn't right. Magnus pushed her back into the arms of Sawyer and swung open the door. Mr. Thompson was hurrying away when Magnus raised his handgun and fired twice. A crack sounded and the thin, elderly man hit the ground about a yard from the main road. Magnus turned back toward Maggie and slapped her across the face. "Do you really take me for an idiot?"

Call it his bullshit meter or just a gut feeling, but when he saw him hurrying away, he figured Maggie had tipped him off even if she didn't say it outright. The question was how? He had an idea.

"What?" Maggie asked, tears rolling down her cheeks.

Magnus didn't wait there to explain. He walked outside because the old man was still alive. He was squirming on his belly in pain, his hands and feet slapping the gravel driveway as he tried to crawl away. As soon as Magnus reached him he placed a foot on his back and the old guy groaned.

"You don't have a son, do you?"

The old man had blood coming out of his mouth.

Magnus stooped down and pressed the muzzle against his temple. "Send God my regards!"

The round echoed loudly. As he returned to the house, Magnus gestured with a thumb over his shoulder for his men to drag the guy into the bushes.

* * *

Rayna was two houses away when she heard the gun. While she was aware that her neighbors were carrying weapons, she was pretty damn sure that gunfire originated from her home.

"Lily, Evan. Back. Now!"

They crossed into the closest driveway. She pulled the rifle off her back and told Lily to take Kong. Since Elliot had returned he'd told her to remain on alert. If in doubt, pull out, as it was better to be safe than sorry. She directed her kids toward the tree line that hedged in the home and they made their way across four property lines before they got back on the road and started heading the other way. As she passed a few neighbors, she asked them if they'd heard any shooting in the area throughout the day. It was possible that someone was just firing off rounds nearby but her gut told her something else.

While speaking to her neighbor Clive Robins, a dark vehicle approached. As it got closer, it pulled off to the edge of the road and that's when she spotted Jesse in the back.

"Jesse? Where's the truck?"

A look of concern spread across his face. "Rayna, have you been home yet?"

"No, I was just heading that way when I heard gunfire."

Damon got out the other side and put his Ruger 22 on top of the car and patted the trunk. "Open up, Amos."

"Would you mind the paint and get your gun off the top?"

"Ah put a sock in it."

The trunk opened, and he pulled out a ballistic vest.

"You want to tell me what's going on? And who are these people?"

Jesse was about to tell her when the driver got out with

a large cigar in his mouth; he looked like a thin version of Boss Hogg from *The Dukes of Hazzard* minus the white threads. He wandered around the back of the vehicle and started harping at Damon for not listening. Damon's expression was dead serious.

"Damon?"

Jesse took a hold of Rayna's arm. "Did you see anyone there?"

"No. I… What is going on?"

"They've got Maggie."

"Who has?"

He sighed. "You remember those guys that attacked you? They were the cousins of a guy in Keene called Magnus. An old friend of Damon's."

"He was no friend," Damon said, correcting him as he came around and slipped into the ballistic vest.

"Rayna, you know these people?" Clive asked looking at them with his hand on his holster.

"Yeah, they're fine."

"Anyway, they're here to avenge Trent. They're here

for Elliot," Damon said.

"Elliot's not here," Rayna said.

"Where is he?"

She shrugged looking at her kids who looked equally perplexed. She turned to Clive. "Clive, do you think you and your wife could keep an eye on my kids for a while until I can figure out what's going on here?"

"Yeah, that's not a problem. Come on, guys," he said beckoning them farther down the road. Clive and his wife, Wendy, lived six homes down. She'd got to know them through her time working at the museum. Clive and Wendy's, eldest child worked in admin.

"Mom," Evan said.

"It's okay, just take Kong and stay put. I'm going to find your father."

She watched them walk off with Clive, a look of reluctance and fear on their faces. Satisfied they were safe she turned her attention back to the four of them. "How many are there?"

"I don't know exactly. Three, maybe more?"

"You're not thinking of going in there, are you?"

"We've got to get Maggie out."

"No, we need to find Elliot and Gary."

Damon pulled the gun off the car. "There is no time. We need to do this now."

"He's right," Jesse said. Rayna took a deep breath and tried to calm her nerves as she mentally prepared to take more lives. It didn't get any easier, but this went beyond saving Maggie, it was about taking back what was hers — her home.

* * *

There were multiple stab wounds to his stomach, and his throat had been slit. Elliot stared at Ted Murphy's corpse. Not long after taking back the Olympic Center, they were about to leave for the north end to investigate the arson incidents when Officer Jackson's radio came alive with a call from Terri Boyd, an office administrator who worked for Mayor Hammond. She was acting all hysterical, barely able to string two words together without bawling her eyes out. All they were able to extract from the blubbering mess was a name — Foster Goodman.

Instead of going north, they sent Jackson and the volunteer while they returned to the town hall in the hopes of finding Goodman; instead they found Ted's body, and another dead officer.

It was no ordinary death; Ted had died in a frenzied attack.

They figured the officer who was assigned to watch over the department and town hall officials must have got caught off-guard as he had a single bullet to the temple and was slumped down as if Goodman had been in waiting.

According to Terri, she'd been startled by gunfire and emerged from her office just in time to see a bloodied Goodman exit the building leaving behind a wake of devastation. Mayor Hammond was nowhere to be found.

"He's not at home," Gary said after getting off the radio. He stepped into Murphy's office and paused for a second as he looked at the man he'd come to despise.

There was no trace of sympathy in his expression. "Hammond's wife said he had left for the town hall early this morning. Goodman must have him."

"But why not just kill him here?" Elliot muttered to himself. They stood there for a second chewing it over then it dawned on Elliot. "I think I know where he might be."

Chapter 23

Magnus grabbed a clump of Maggie's hair and dragged her down the hallway kicking and screaming. He tossed her into the kitchen and she slid across the floor and collapsed in a heap against a cupboard.

He stooped down and jabbed his finger at her.

"I made it pretty fucking clear what I would do, and I'm a man of my word. He's dead, now so are you."

With that said he turned to Sawyer. "Take her into the bunker and teach her some manners, and when you're done, kill her."

Maggie couldn't believe what they were saying. It was like having an out-of-body experience. Magnus turned away. She screamed cowering back in fear as Sawyer approached. "No. No!"

He took a grip of her wrist and tried to drag her but she began fighting back. As she was doing this Tyron was bargaining with Magnus to let him be the one to handle her. While their backs were turned, her fight-or-flight instincts kicked in and she drove her foot into Sawyer's knee and he buckled letting out an agonized cry. She scrambled across the kitchen floor like a wounded gazelle fleeing from a predator. Her heart hammered in her chest. Every inch she got closer to the back door was one step closer to freedom. That freedom never came. She felt a hard thud at the back of her head and collapsed in a heap. Now all she could see and hear was fragments of her reality, a mishmash of voices and then her body shifting across the ground.

* * *

From the cover of the dense forest that hedged in the home, Damon and the others looked on assessing the situation. They'd heard screaming and Jesse wanted to move in but both Damon and Amos had to hold him back. What came next shocked them all. The back door swung open and Sawyer emerged dragging Maggie across the yard toward the bunker. Jesse brought up his rifle but Damon slapped it down. "You want to kill her?"

"Look at her!" Jesse jabbed his finger forward as Sawyer disappeared into the shed.

"We'll get her but your shooting accuracy isn't that great and there are too goddamn many of them to go rushing out there."

"Well you better think fast or I'm going in."

"No you're not."

"You gonna stop me?" Jesse said.

"If I have to."

Rayna intervened. "Enough!"

They turned their attention back to the house. From what Damon could see, the rest were inside. His mind went into overdrive. Storming the house wasn't an option, and he knew Magnus well enough to know that he wasn't going to stand out in the open. He was crazy but not that crazy. As they crouched in the underbrush trying to figure out the best approach, Damon heard movement from the rear. He twisted around bringing his rifle up only to find Clive Robins and two other armed men.

Clive threw his hands up. "Whoa, we thought you could use some help."

As they spoke with Rayna, Damon spotted something in the yard that gave him an idea. He turned to Clive and the other two. "You want to help? Come with me."

"What are you doing?" Rayna asked.

"You'll see. Just be ready to take them out."

He turned to Jesse. "Take my father and circle around. Go get her!"

Damon turned to Amos. "I need the keys to your car."

"Over my dead body."

"Look, old man, I don't have time for your bullshit right now. Let's go."

Amos looked reluctant but with everyone staring at him he buckled under the pressure. "You put one scratch on my baby and heads are gonna roll."

"Yeah, yeah," Damon said snatching up the keys before jogging off at a crouch with Clive and two other neighbors. He came to learn their names were Brian and Thomas. When they made it out of the forest into the backyard of the next home, he hurried over to a BBQ and started to detach the propane tank.

"We're going to need at least three of these. Go check some of the other houses. Be quick."

They sprinted away while he lugged the propane tank down the driveway and over to the Caddy. He popped the passenger door open, pulled the seat forward so there was hardly any room in the front and jammed the tank between the seat and the dashboard. In the distance he heard gunfire. He hoped to God that Jesse was doing what he told him. Next, he opened the trunk and fished around for the breakdown kit Amos had stuck in the back. Beyond the usual crap that could be found like an air compressor for flat tires, jumper cables, a 12-foot towrope, gloves, warning triangle and first-aid kit, were two road flares. He took them out. A few minutes later, Clive and the others returned with three canisters.

"Good, load two of them into the passenger side."

They stacked them haphazardly on top of each other and then closed the door. Damon took the last one and reared it back and used it to smash out the passenger window. He them jammed the tank inside with half of it exposed.

"Head back and circle around the west side and provide support."

They nodded and dashed off toward the home while he hopped into the driver's side and fired up the engine. Damon tore away from the hard shoulder and then swerved, parking the car with the front end facing the front of Rayna's driveway. The car idled as he hopped out and dashed over to the edge of the road and rummaged around in the undergrowth for a solid, thick branch. He broke off the limbs and snapped it over his leg until it was the right size and then headed back to the car. He knew he'd only get one shot at this. Damon jammed the branch between the bottom of the seat and the accelerator. The gearstick was still in park. As soon as the branch connected with the accelerator it started revving loudly. The wheels spun, kicking up dirt and smoke. He partially sat in the vehicle so he could engage the brake, align the wheels and then shift the gearstick into drive. Before doing that he took the two road flares, removed the cap from one, then struck the cap's rough surface on the end of the flare. A golden flame about three inches long burst forth, fizzling and blowing in the breeze. He did the same with the next and then jammed them between the propane tanks with the flame facing up. Damon shifted the gearstick into drive, dived out and rolled as the mint-condition, black, 1949 Cadillac shot forward heading straight for the house. Damon scrambled to get up and dashed into the tree line, his eyes swept the scene as he watched the vehicle speed down the driveway and collide at an angle into the brick and clapboard home. He'd expected the whole thing to explode but nothing happened. Windows shattered, metal crunched, and a portion of the front end embedded in the home but that was it. Nothing but the sound of an engine revving, and the flares fizzling.

"What the hell did you do?" Amos yelled running up to meet him. Before he got close enough to verbally or physically assault him, Damon took aim at the partially exposed propane tank and squeezed off a round. It didn't immediately explode but a huge ten-foot blue flame shot out of the side. The second round tore through it, igniting and causing an eruption of epic proportion.

The fifteen-foot explosion tore through the front of the home. Every window in the front of the house shattered, and golden tongues of fire licked up the upper portion of the house enveloping it in a cloud of smoke and flames.

* * *

Minutes earlier, Maggie was shoved into the living area; her body collided with a small coffee table. Sawyer leered at her, the corner of his mouth turning. He walked over and slapped her across the face twice causing her to cry out in pain.

"Oh I'm going to enjoy this."

He then started unbuckling his pants.

"Let's get acquainted."

Blood was trickling down the side of her face as she

reached for the nearest object, a vase full of fake flowers, she tossed it at him but he ducked and then let out a laugh.

"Feisty, I like that."

He extracted his belt and snapped it a few times to intimidate her. Maggie scrambled back trying to escape him but he was on her fast, pushing her to the floor and clamping his legs around her body. He wrapped the belt around her neck in a noose and began to twist. A flash of memories from her ex-boyfriend beating her rushed through her mind — his face and a continual wave of pain. Maggie gasped then fired back driving her fist as hard as she could into Sawyer's solar plexus. Elliot had taught her a thing or two while down in that bunker, one of which was points on the body that could disable an attacker.

Hit them in just the right spot and it doesn't matter how big they are, they will go down.

As her fist connected with his solar plexus, Sawyer gasped. Before he could take his next breath, she jammed her palm up under his nose bursting it, then grabbed his arm, four fingers in from the elbow, and dug her thumb into it while pulling him off. She followed through with a finger jab to the eye. Sawyer collapsed to one side but still wasn't completely off her. He groaned in agony, reaching for his nose and eye. Maggie struggled to slip out and climb over his legs. She'd nearly done it when he clamped on to the back of her shirt and dragged her down, banging her head against the hard steel.

"You fucking bitch!"

He threw a punch and cracked her in the temple causing her to almost black out. When she regained her senses, he'd shifted position and had one knee up and the other on the floor. He was trying to control the bleeding from his nose while at the same time adjusting the belt around her neck. She knew she had minutes before he would kill her.

In that instant, an explosion startled him. It was so loud he instinctively twisted in the direction it was coming from. That's when she saw the blade again. In one smooth move she snapped the button on the side and yanked it out. Feeling her grasp it, he turned to react, but it was too late, she jammed that knife into the side of his neck screaming at the top of her lungs at the same time. "Die, you bastard!"

Sawyer's eyed widened; he clamped on to the knife and began gasping as he staggered back. She had to have pierced the jugular as blood was squirting out the side of his neck like a fountain.

"Maggie!"

She heard Jesse's voice.

Chapter 24

"Come on! Come on!" Damon said as he worked his way around the side of the house waiting for Magnus to show. He raked the muzzle of his rifle back and forth. Nothing moved across his field of vision. Black and gray smoke billowed out of windows. They wouldn't be able to stay in there long.

Meanwhile, Amos was yelling in his ear about his car.

"That car was priceless. Do you hear me?"

Without even looking at him he replied, "Old man, you are really getting on my tits! Shut the hell up before I put you in the ground."

"I'd like to see that. This is going to cost you."

"Yeah, send the bill in the mail."

An individual burst out coughing and spluttering, his eyes wild and full of fear. He turned to run back but before he'd even made it a few feet, he took a round to the back and collapsed. Damon's eyes darted to the tree line east of them and saw the muzzle of Clive's gun sticking out. There was a fleeting moment of silence before the real gunfire started. Under the gray sky and low daylight conditions it was easy to see the muzzle flashes from two of the windows in the rear. Bullets tore up the dirt near Clive even as they returned fire. Magnus had sacrificed one of his own as a means to find out where his attackers were. On the south side where they were positioned, no one was firing at them, which meant he either had no clue they were there or he was waiting for them to emerge. Damon hurried over to Rayna who was taking cover behind a tree. She'd positioned herself at an angle and was waiting patiently for a target.

Rounds speared into tree trunks sending bark spitting in every direction. Behind the safety of the trees he surveyed the property, considering every possible escape option. As the flames engulfed the front of the home, he knew it was only a matter of time before they were forced out. It was either that or they would die of smoke inhalation.

Damon tapped Rayna on the shoulder. "I'm going around the north side, it's the only area we don't have covered. Stay here, okay? They stick their head out…"

"Take them out. I know," she replied, her face a picture of concentration.

Damon turned to Amos. "Okay, old man, time to show us what you're capable of — let's go!"

"I'm not going anywhere with you."

"Suit yourself."

Rayna pressed her back to the tree. "Just back him up."

"He ruined my vehicle."

Amos looked like he'd spent too much time cooped up in his home. His problem wasn't with Damon, it was with anyone telling him what to do.

"He ruined my house, so I think that trumps your heap of shit. Now go before I put a bullet in your ass," she replied. Either he liked her comeback, or he was genuinely afraid of her but he fell in step.

* * *

Elliot punched the gas pedal and sped toward the intersection near Saranac Avenue and Mirror Lake. He was going on a gut feeling and there was a chance he was wrong on the location, but it was the only thing that made sense.

Gary tossed his hands up. "Slow down, where are we heading?"

"Do you remember two years ago, Foster lost a son in a collision?"

"Vaguely."

"Vaguely?" Elliot repeated.

"I don't read a lot of news, Elliot."

"Geesh!" Elliot shook his head. "It was the talk of the town."

"Yeah, well I've never been one for gossip."

"Anyway, he blamed Wayland, and filed a civil lawsuit against him and the department due to the way things were handled. He wasn't the only one raising accusations against him."

"That, I remember."

"Foster said that Wayland's wife was to blame and that he'd been involved in covering it up."

"So you think Foster killed him?"

"That's my guess."

"And what about Bolton, and the fires?"

"Nothing more than a distraction."

Elliot swerved onto Main Street and weaved his way around stalled vehicles. In the distance smoke rose above buildings, another reminder of society collapsing in on itself. As they got closer to the intersection he spotted Goodman, holding a handgun in one hand and dragging Hammond with the other. He slammed on the brakes, which let out a muffled screech as he took the Jeep up onto the curb so they could take cover behind a row of vehicles. Goodman looked in their direction and fired off two rounds, one shattered the windshield sending shards of glass inward.

"Shit!" Elliot stabbed the brake again, killed the engine, then pushed out of the vehicle and dropped to the ground with his AR-15. Another flurry of rounds peppered the vehicles they were taking cover behind and punched through glass.

"Goodman, you don't want to do this!" Gary yelled.

Elliot moved around a vehicle and crouched next to the back end of a 4 x 4 truck. Elliot risked a glance around the rear. Foster saw him and squeezed off three more rounds. The bullets took out a tire, and it let out a steady hiss.

Pulling back, he and Gary stayed low inching their way up to the front end. Elliot darted to the next vehicle and peered through the window of a Ford. Mayor Hammond had a noose around his neck and the other end was strung over the top of one of the tall overarching lampposts. Even though Hammond was struggling to get loose, Foster would just strike him with the butt of his gun. His head was streaming with blood.

"Keep him busy while I take the shot."

He expected Gary to tell him to hold off, but he didn't this time. Elliot figured he knew the only way to handle this now was to kill him before Hammond was strung up.

Elliot shuffled up to the front end of the Ford and swung his rifle over the top, resting it on the hood just as Goodman tried to get the mayor to stand on a small footstool. He had to have prepared it ahead of time as there was no way he could have set it up and controlled Hammond at the same time.

Gary shouted, "Listen to me, Foster. It doesn't need to end this way."

"Of course it does. He's as much to blame as Wayland. They're all to blame."

Gary looked over to Elliot who brought his eye up to the scope but had to pull back as Foster spotted him and opened fire. Bullets ricocheted off metal. Elliot ducked down. Foster turned his gun toward Hammond and instructed him to get up onto the stool.

"Get up. Do it now!"

A few more rounds in their direction and Elliot knew it was now or never. He swung the rifle over and Foster locked eyes with him. Foster tried to fire off another round but was out. Hammond lunged forward into him, and Gary used the moment to dash forward. Elliot didn't bother to wait, he wasn't going to let him live. He brought his eye to the scope, even as Gary shouted for him to not take the shot.

Too late.

The gun let out a crack.

The round struck Foster in the chest and spun him to the ground.

* * *

Magnus had lost control of the situation. It happened so fast. One minute he was envisioning the future, the next coughing his lungs out from all the smoke. He'd instructed Tyron to push one of his group out in order to determine where they were. While he hadn't seen them he assumed it was Elliot. How many were out there? One, two, maybe more? He'd had another one of his guys try to exit the south side but he had come under heavy fire. The only way out was the rear door or north side through a small bathroom window.

"Tyron! Send them out," Magnus yelled.

"They won't go."

Magnus was looking out the bathroom window when Tyron replied. Smoke was filling up the house, drifting through the rooms. He could feel the heat and hear the sound of wood crackling and items dropping to the ground. He coughed hard and lifted his top over his mouth as he emerged with a Glock raised. "Get out there now or I'll kill you here."

"No."

He didn't waste a second punching a bullet through the guy's skull. They meant nothing to him. They were just a means to an end and under the circumstances the only thing that made sense was escaping. He shifted the Glock to the next guy, and Tyron did the same with the other. They brought up their hands, fear splashed across their faces as they darted toward the door and hurried out in a hail of gunfire.

"Let's go." Magnus led the way into the bathroom and popped the window up and shimmied out, dropping to the ground. Tyron followed as Magnus hurried into the tree line.

* * *

Damon spotted Magnus as he rushed out into the driveway that hugged the north side of the house. He raised his weapon but didn't get the shot off in time. He disappeared into the coverage of the forest. Tyron wasn't as lucky.

Pop!

He dropped him with a shot to the side of his chest. Damon took off in pursuit while shouting at Amos to finish Tyron off. He ducked into the dense cluster of pines and oaks in time to see Magnus darting in and out. Damon pointed his AR-15 and got off three shots sending Magnus diving for cover behind a tree.

* * *

Magnus reached down and gripped the side of his stomach, then brought up a hand gloved in blood. He took a peek around the corner of the tree and could see Damon making his way over. He squeezed off a few shots to hold him off. His breathing became heavy. "You sonofabitch!"

"You didn't have to kill her, Magnus."

He let out a chuckle. "You're still thinking about her? Shit man, whatever happened to bros before hoes?"

Damon didn't reply. Magnus could hear him getting close. He knew he wasn't going to make it out of that forest. He was bleeding out badly. Fear gripped him. He didn't want to die. This wasn't how it was meant to end.

He brought the Glock around and fired off three more rounds, each one speared into the tree Damon was behind. He struggled to get up and jog to the next tree. At least if he had to die, he wasn't going to give him the satisfaction of taking his life without a fight. He released his magazine and palmed another one into place before bringing a round into the chamber.

"You know what, Damon. It's been one hell of a ride, hasn't it?"

He turned and looked back but couldn't see him. His eyes frantically scanned his field of vision. His mouth was dry, and his hands shook. He was starting to feel cold from blood loss. He tilted his head trying hard to listen for his movements but there was nothing. Then a twig snapped, and another at the sound of boots rushing forward. He twisted around the other side of the tree directly into the bullet.

Epilogue

A bright morning sun bathed the snow-brushed mountains over Lake Placid as Elliot and Rayna picked through what remained of their home. A chilly breeze swept ash across the yard. Although the bunker was still intact, it seemed that almost all their photos, memories and belongings had gone up in smoke. He kicked at the charred wood and searched for anything of sentimental value. Beneath the blanket of destroyed belongings, he spotted a family photo that had made it. Though the glass frame was partially melted and soot hid the image, it was still intact for the most part. He wiped away the grime with his sleeve and then shattered the glass so he could retrieve the snapshot.

It was just a memory but now that was all they had, and it meant a lot.

"You never hit him?" Rayna asked.

"I wanted to."

"What stopped you?"

He sighed. "I'm not sure, to be honest."

"Have you seen him?"

"Nope. He said he needed to talk to her."

Rayna nodded. "Yeah, I tried but she wouldn't listen."

"Do you blame her?"

She breathed in deeply.

"No. I just miss my old friend."

There was a moment of silence.

"Me too."

Rayna eyed him as they continued searching.

"Tell me something. Why did you believe me?" she asked.

He paused and tossed a charred piece of wood and contemplated the question. "I'd like to say it's because you're my wife and I know you better than anyone else, and while that's true... the way I see it — under the circumstances, you had no reason to lie. If ever there was a justified reason to cut ties, it would have been then when I had nothing to give you except my problems."

Rayna nodded slowly before reaching for his hand.

A couple of days after rescuing Maggie, the group buried Mr. Thompson in a marked grave at the back of his home. His elderly wife, Gail, was so devastated that Gary brought her together with other victims of society's collapse in the hope she'd draw comfort and strength from those in the same pain. As hard as it was to see the suffering, it was a sign of the times. All of them bore scars in different ways, some physical, most emotional.

After spending some time with Damon, Buddy and Amos headed back to Keene, believing they could scrape together enough to ride out the unknown. For a day or so, Damon had considered going with them but at the last moment chose to stay. While Maggie was being treated for an infection at the local medical center, Jesse remained at her side having become close through the harrowing ordeal.

So much had changed since New York, not just in them but in the community at large.

The future was uncertain. Tomorrow was a gamble.

But family remained the same, and that was worth fighting for.

Over two weeks in an EMP had taught them many lessons, most of which had cost them dearly. But through the confusion, violence and desperation of a country without power, two things had become very clear — no one was an island, and a community was only as strong as those willing to sacrifice.

* * *

THANK YOU FOR READING

Days of Chaos: (Book 2)

Days of Danger will be out soon

Please take a second to leave a review, it's really

appreciated. Thanks kindly, Jack.

A Plea

Thank you for reading Days of Chaos. If you enjoyed the book, I would really appreciate it if you would consider leaving a review. Without reviews, an author's books are virtually invisible on the retail sites. It also lets me know what you liked. You can leave a review by visiting the book's page. I would greatly appreciate it. It only takes a couple of seconds.

Thank you — **Jack Hunt**

Newsletter

Thank you for buying Days of Chaos, published by Direct Response Publishing.

Click here to receive special offers, bonus content, and news about new Jack Hunt's books. Sign up for the newsletter. http://www.jackhuntbooks.com/signup/

About the Author

Jack Hunt is the author of horror, sci-fi and post-apocalyptic novels. He currently has three books out in the War Buds Series, Two books in the Wild Ones series, three in the Camp Zero series, five books out in the Renegades series, three books in the Agora Virus series, one called Blackout, one called Final Impact, one called Darkest Hour, one out in the Armada series, a time travel book called Killing Time and another called Mavericks: Hunters Moon. Jack lives on the East coast of North America.

Made in the USA
Columbia, SC
30 December 2018